Zak Ferguson

we +

you

= us

Hardcover version ISBN: 9798871115435

Paperback version ISBN: 9798871522974

we + you = us

we + you = us

Zak Ferguson

we

We plus you equals us.

We plus the old me and the old you equals totality.

We were empty on our own.

We are now one.

We are a whole.

We came together the moment the nucleus event occurred.

We as the nucleus event as seen as an event horizon.

We as the fading out, the disappearance, witnessed, and experienced.

We are the inside and outside of it.

We are the unmanageable percentages tallied in bunkers in Texas, broken down, all so a lesser life-form can later surmise, *Hmmmm, that's interesting,* putting on faux expressions, trying to pass themselves off as something they are not, and can never be.

We read between the lines, separately.

We were two different beings with two different copies of the same book; one in mint condition, the other paged through as if it were a manual on how to be the world's best lover; worn, sticky, crispy in certain spots/chapters; as soon as we pieced together different verses, stanzas, prose alignments, that were put there to be moved around and about, we found each other so we could become....

We, us, as a whole.

We were two different "people", that is how these things work. On Earth. In these paradoxical terms we have to get used to whilst studying at school, to attain grades that will do nada for our self-esteem or ego; but apparently will do a lot for our futures; paying off costly loans, never attaining grants because our art, our vision isn't good enough.

We are not up to scratch.

We are here.

We are there.

We transmuted the *us* of *before* so we could then alter those around *us* - solely for personal, irrational, physics-altering, selfish "reasons", all so the me turned into the us, into the we stood out better in society.

We move as one.

We moved as one.

We always used to feel as if our own identities stood out from ourselves.

We knew some part of our DNA, our kernel of self that existed in similar disrepair, that was waiting on the other side of the road, per se, for the other's identity shadow to conjoin and make *us* of before a unified *us*.

We became *we*.

We were the frozen breaths left to hang upon the summit of Everest, comingling with all the other last breaths exhaled from supposed great adventurers and mountain climbers.

We moved amongst the breaths of all that did and did not reach the peak. The apex was conquered by the last breaths of Alexander Mitchell Kellas, the Unknown Porter, Dorje, Lhakpa, Norbu, Passang, Perma, Sange, Temba, Man Bahadur, Lance-Naik, Andrew Irvine, Geroge Mallory.

We travelled to the furthest reaches of our planet only to witness that it never ends, it stretches on.

We do not believe in a flat Earth.

We do believe that all flat earthers deserve to be flattened beneath the wheels of a chariot rode into battle, or some wanky-ceremony with Gaius Appuleius Diocleswe holding onto the reins.

We believe in the ball.

We accept that we are trapped within the globe.

We are part and parcel of the planetoid that we reside on.

We think that this still doesn't mean we are not existing on a blackhole turned malleable and constructive. Planet Praxis rippling out into the never-ending, not so yellow brick road.

We are the minor imperfections.

We are inflections of mirrored images slowed, sped up, layered, burnt into each other .

We are the time-delay, the curls of vapour, beautiful colours unrecorded and unseen by human eyes, we are those colours, and we are also the witnesses of such colours.

We are the cloudscape undulating out into the darkness of space.

We are these things, and what that means is, that what is offered to us a comprehension-dilation fragment - presenting how our planet functions in the molasses of information and unreality that govern our universe, is merely unimagined; that of which is unimagined cannot exist as a certainty.

We are a form of realism made unrealistic.

We need you to sit at a fashionable desk and try and extract cubist compositions.

We need you to go to your local fleapit cinema. Fleapit meaning an age-old staple of a local town. Many have them. Many do not.

We want you to make a detour and visit this place.

We know there is one.

We know it is close. Geographically and emotionally.

We need you to concede to our ushering.

We want you to go to the neglected, occasionally accepted, but never supported or visited palace of old. Previously left to the local avant-garde artists and punk poet scenes; vomit still left where it landed and dried. A place where no film has been screened in the past few years, a grand theatre of old.

We know this is true paradise.

We know you like it.

We know that perhaps the place is closed up. Shuttered. Boarded up. Left to its own demise. Falling into itself. Even the local shysters and street bumpers and snorters and slanderers merely cover under the balcony – conceal, sleep, hide, junk up, but they never transfer their filth beyond the balcony's perpetually left open facade. The old poster boxes are also lovingly wiped by the dirtbags; tiles smashed, uptilted, hastily out of a weird sense of propriety by the street sleepers, zombie walkers, whilst the rest is an open prison cell, littered with used needles, broken bottles, stubbed out roll-ups, and filthy sleeping bags in various stages of disintegration.

We prod you.

We guide you.

We force you.

We prod you.

We force you.

We goad you.

We want you to follow us.

We make sure you follow the cinema song, into the cinema of the old days. The kind with beautifully sculpted cornices, the serge fire retardant curtains, that are forever pulled close, never opened to reveal the fragile old cinema screen, that is marred by various mosquito and moth assaults, marked by insect-suicide; a vast plethora of light attracted insects and some people, who ended up splattered into and onto the screen - attracted to its ambient light; now left to their spastic devices in the rafters; not the humans (or maybe some reside up there in spirit) this fleapit has a proscenium stage, set up as a barrier between audience and the screen – also a staple of these types òf establishments; this theatre, this "fleapit" that was ahead of the curve, that deserves your reverential self. The building standing out in all its antiquarian grandeur, that stood out as an example of how advanced they were in the early days of the past we can only track by restorative Blu-ray re-releases.

We want you to ease into this place. Admire. Feel. Extend. Project. Flicker. In. Out. In and out. In/Out. Burn delightfully. A sense of feeling. A taste of feeling. Salty. Sweet. Buttery. Musky. Piss. Vinegar. Roasted nuts. Polished vinyl. Bleach. Antiseptic wipes. The taste of soul. The taste of conjoined genres. The taste of films. A taste of movies as well. The aesthetic. The beauty. The art. The history. The dregs of humanity coming to ease up on their household abuse inhaled like a sweet Mary-jay-jay joint.

We want you to loosen. Just relax. Merge in with the seat. The seats of old. Elderly seats, taking on the aged patrons mid-80s sad sack of lonely shit substance. Rickety, musky seats. The aisles flooring loose, certain boards angled upward, that if you placed a light kid on one end and got a huge fat monster on the other, you'd send the little mite up into the crumbling rafters. Would such an impact bring the rest down? Perhaps. Probably. No, most definitely. The old nuts and bolts holding the aisle of seats down seem to give way, yet never do, they do so love to threaten an upheaval. Always threatening to pop out, and to ruin the rows of varyingly decayed states left leaning like tombstones.

We want you to sit down and try not to wiggle. Feel the material of the cinema seat. The fibres of the torn, fraying vintage coverings, and the fragmenting wooden board that forms such a seat. A seat that forces the non-artists of the world, the dribbling, glassy-eyed dullards to straighten up, pay a-fucking-tension. Position your leg so you can look at the corners – bask in the loneliness, and dead vibe. Look to the left of the row you're seated on, at the end of the row.

We want you to muse on history and to really home in on the ill-gotten additions that the last owner imposed into this sacred arena. Enter the spatial oblongs that created such a zone. Witness the seats that could at any minute fall like dominoes, or be uplifted with a person, if they rush up in haste to get some popcorn or to take a leak, like those tiny school chairs you are forced in when going to Parents Evening; it comes away with you, and as these seats that have been cheaply drilled, pathetically/hastily "Fixed" they will come as a row, with your own personal butt-squeezer; taking some of cinema-palaces past back home with you.

We tune into the stereo speakers.

We play creepy music.

We want you to experience various sensory incursions of your cine-trapped self. Funny music. Sad music. Then, the visuals play across the screen.

We bring cinema in increments.

We know you have the skill to piece it together and later on, alone in your bedroom, whether still living with Mum and Dad, or a house share, you'll re-edit it, correctly, wrongly, or experimentally.

We are subhuman.

We are nonplussed over the words we produce in hope it will leave an indelible mark on the white spaces in-between human experience.

We know the movie you create will bring the house down.

We send you letters. Inside these letters are snapshots of our own personal favourite haunts of old.

We love them.

We know you will too.

We ask you to do us a favour; please, in any way that you can, please frame them.

We especially love the house of lords cinema room.

We want you to notice why this set up makes little to no sense, in a cinema-viewing way. The whole surreal nature of its architecture and setup makes it utterly unique, and rather beguiling.

We are fully formed fuck ups.

We are the sum of everything the other has done.

We are combined.

We are oneself, though we exist as separate beings.

We are both male & female.
We are contradictions.

We contradictions like to call ourselves *subversions.*

We the great subverters, *but of what?*

We are *just*, and as we are *just* you must shut the fuck up and get back in line.

We sit in stranger's gardens and read to one another.

We are weaponizing manifestos left to rot.

We read backwards, speaking in tongues, changing syllables for numbers and numbers for grunts.

We have created our own method of communication.

We have done this because who can stop us?

We share a mind.

We share a form.

We do not share a body.

We have used stranger's gardens for other things other than reading and misquoting Antonin Artaud quotes.

We spoke only so we could then be silenced by the ubiquitous permutations of unnamed, uncared for, uncalled for, gu, gu, gu, gu-ods!

"We must wash literature off ourselves. We want to be men above all, to be human, and above the aforementioned the above, that is the above to all, to be an us, a we, and thus being the purest of forms, the us of then and never."

We invite the owner to join us, and only end up getting led of the premises by so local bobby-boi.

"We never tire ourselves more than   is essentially inessential, even if you have to found a culture on the fatigue of your bone-dust."

We read to each other even when we don't like the other's choice of book to read.

We read because we want to *autodidact* ourselves.

We only want to *autodidact*, and not, let's say, *self-educate,* because being an *autodidact* is cultish.

We comb the moonlit shopping fronts. Flitting by. Flit flit flit flit flit flit flit flit.

We admire the zoetrope-fashion we have designed by running past moonlit, lamplit, interiorly self-lit storefronts.

We walk.

We run.

We are heading towards some uncircumcised trial.

We await the gavel.

We will tear the judges clothes off in front of the jury in front of the world as everything must be televised and as we abuse the morbidly obsess judge's moobs we move onto his arsehole.

We anally probe the judge, fingering his ass, enjoying the break of his ass-hymen, admiring his screams of terror – terraforming his internal system as our cock slides in with our natural cock-lubricant easing the insertion and prodding/probing/injecting of our masterfully ordinary phallus.

We pummel into the anus and the terraformed judge produces sweet erotic melodies and doodahs! His mouth making the anus splash, foaming from his mouth, brown bubbles, and flaking ass-scrum caught on his lower lip and chin.

We purposefully pur-*poise* our rugged selves.

We bask in the lunar reflections.

We neglect that - the lunar - reflections are a filtration of the real hard-core rays of energy.

We are vain, so we cannot not look at ourselves as the lunar rays pierce our bodies and break us down, bit by bit, X-ray vision, with the added cult tang of potential radiation poisoning, because we are vain.

We are happy to be unhappy.

We are unhappy when not possessing the bonhomie of old.

We are writers without doing any verily appropriate writing.

We think.

We know that is enough.

We think.

We drink the gospels, admire the old masters.

We use the New Testament and Old Testament and The In-Between Testament, as tiles to our non-existing kitchenette.

We trace the veins of each other's and our own hands.

We are romantic.

We are sophisticatedly banal, that banal becomes hackneyed, hackneyed becomes stale, stale becomes null and totally fucking void.

We are lovers.

We dance over our corpse.

We were great obliterators of the literary scene that neither of us felt totally comfortable in.

We land in a puddle that teleports us into a garden on the other side of town, our backward reentry into the familiar is assward.

We buried our bodies.

We together buried our old selves.

We did things to the bodies, our bodies, that would make Fred West blush, and Rose West maniacally finger herself over in total befuddlement and arousal.

We know Rose does it out of a weird sense of self preservation.

We were writers. Plurally. Singularly. Lies.

We were grunts, grease monkeys, plumbers, office drones, film directors, French critics, French only because we acquired a fancy beret, or is it fez?

We were advanced for our ages combined.

We are the Post Modernist's wet dream.

We are the Surrealists unfortunate cancer diagnosis.

We are the shamanic cures that failed to save Kathy Acker.

We are Francis Bacon's oozing swelling.

We were troubled.

We were skint.

We were applying for various grants and then opted for loans, merely so we could neglect the repayments.

We became surveyors, of our own warped made-up business.

We hate vapes.

We targeted vapers, who let their little finger daintily point out as if they had been schooled in The British School of Excellence, knowing full well they couldn't pronounce the word *aesthetics* properly without their Aldi co-worker saying it over and over, making out that he himself was of a certain creed and position; when we all know, an Aldi worker is an Aldi worker for a reason – and we willed their vapes to explode.

We witnessed carnage.

We dope.

We smoke.

We bump.

We hump.

We introduce ourselves as not they, or them, or xe, but as we.

The modern world cannot accept us unless they have created a pronoun for us to apply ourselves to.

We grind it altogether to create the loveliest of moistures to transfer in our adapted infuser.

We merge together without ever having to merge.

We were one from the start, circling eagles, readied to attack only to keep up this sky-dance until the atoms knocked on the door and exclaimed, "BOOM!"

We are above Aldi, Asda, Morrison, Sainsbury's workers.

We rebel.

We retaliate.

We work work work work work, hard at dossing.

We cut up your phrases and words and the emotions behind it all.

We hear, bless, um, are, a lot more, Matt, they are, scared of you, it's weird, actually, not that, wouldn't, imagine, personal, I said, well, (laughter), share, she, yeah-um, don't, I, Uh, Elizabeth, working, people, got to, individual, absolutely-absolutely, (giggles) no, level, of, no, not, very, I, you know, dare, terrified, adding, not included, hehehe, terrified of adding extra, going on, as it is, it is, a huge, nothing to do with, but, wow, how on Earth, um, hehehe, I think, only, I think, scared of you, for me, doing transport, in my eyes, said, aren't being approved, have to come to me, should have, felt, going to email, going up and above, smokers, little, killed her with a heart attack hehehe, har!

We are evolutionary babies.

We run amok in the wake of a world full of spinsters, abusers, politicians left in social experiments.

We are in an art room.

We are the art restoration.

We are the frames.

We are the paints.

We are Francis Bacon's swollen face after being hornily assaulted.

We coo to the Bacon of old.

We cry.

We splice open the bruise from the inside and spill all of Bacon's lovers guts, all of the users and financial abusers.

We are visiting many low-key events where avant-garde is made TikTok important.

We hate TikTok-ers.

We exist in a world made up of sin, sin so sinful it is now no longer sinful, just conditioning.

We are evolution.

We put our fingers into frying pan and watch as our fingers crisp in the oil.

We admire smells like film critics admire Michael Bay movies in secret.

We exist in a world come undone where man-babies are crying for their non-existent Mammies, fighting other morbidly obese man babies, petulant, pathetic slaps and eventual torrents of shit-pissing and piss-shitting, and shit-foaming, the shit leaking from their overflowing man-diapers, the freshest stream struggling to wash away the thirty-day shit-caked thigh encasers, hardened like a cast, all because man-babies had gone unwiped and un-licked for longer than a few weeks; shit-licker's are on the case, kind of, on all fours, arses bent high in the air, weird postures that toddlers learning to walk position, or the types of people P. T Barnum liked to exploit; weird praying mantis arms propelling themselves ever onward, legs dragging behind, though they seem pointless, they lent to the surreal misshapen look of their ilk; an ilk constantly chasing the man-babies of this evolutionarily fucked world that we created by not obeying, trailing after them; *why can't they lick up, clean up, nurse man-baby, baby?*

We think, back at you, *don't be so absurd, you nuisances to an authorial voices mythology in the making, stop interrupting, these shit-licker's have as many brains as an American President, those that held office in the years between 1800 to 2040; and retarded pimps wearing Iceberg Slim carbon copy hand-me-downs.*

We came before and after the great devastation.

We contributed on the sidelines.

We catered to the perverse. Our manifestos/pamphlets came from the id and not the physical materialisations that certain people of weak-willed identities and mental

We were the people that didn't want to do this, but we really did want to do this.

We don't want to ruin the illusion, but... they ain't legit pimp materials. Those pimp materials are all cosplay made/designed/imagined. Sad really.

We are the barking dogs of the urban environment, where we are heard, yet never seen. That is for the best. As our bite is perhaps worser than our bark. Woof, bloody woof.

We were inerrant in our targets. Like the delinquent bowling ball we didn't want to strike out, no, no, no.

We wanted to veer to the left, not so close to the runnel's that guide the balls back into position all so they can be recirculated back to us to try and try again; fuck that noise, we think.

We are the sentient bowling ball, curving its way to another aisle, fucking up another person's expertly positioned and arranged shot/bowl.

We had scoured the landscapes of our victims.

We had plunged our different tools into their succulent meat and various placed orifices; some god-made/mam-made; others, by our own invention.

We were vacuum packed into our resolve.

We were united by our mistakes.

We were our concerns, our habits, our vices, our weaknesses, personified in full-bodied, blood splattered, grimy pored throes of heightened instability.

We were on the run.

We are on the run, still.

We are/were forced into each other's orbit, not by mere chance, but the hand of some alternative God that doesn't rhyme with pseudopod.

We are the Übermensch.

We take the philosophy of others, and birth from our awkwardly placed birthing canal, a new, and improved Friedrich. The baby Friedrich is all but a doughy ball, with a distinguished moustache, working as hair, earmuffs, eyebrows, eyelids, like some Miyazaki drawing.

We took a three week my sojourn abroad in the Summer of twenty-twenty-two.

We were hectic.

We did little but sit around, waiting until we could next listen in to what they were getting up to.

We know, that sounds peculiar, and will make one question our aims, and once our age comes into, it will leave one either assuming, *"Oh, well, he is an old busy-body nosy-cunt, there is nothing more to it,"* or you will pair that last thought with the next one, that is that you'll assume we are "some dirty old they, them, getting his/her/their kicks off!"

We have fabricated our involvement in the above.

We have stolen the work of Carl and made it ours.

Well-well, we can't argue against it.

It is true, and we are as shocked by this behaviour as anyone else would (quite rightfully) be.

As much as I plus I equals us, may throughout this story shape it, rationalise it, lend a philosophy and a tortured artist angle to the whole pathetic display, one can't quite deny that this is as much a part of the reasoning behind what we eventually did, in lieu of being introduced into this world of eavesdropping/stalking, than a bored, sad, sexless old creature built out of two separate halves.

We can go one further, a sad, pathetic, loveless creature, who has had their day in the limelight and was now slowly receding into the darkness of an artists self-imposed exile.
We are artists.
We are Hitler's gag reflex.

We are his farts.

We travelled from one end of Europe to another, warning people of his gaseous assaults.

We warned the bomb-makers, the German woman liberators of his slimy touch.

Instead all opposed succumbed to his fruitful farts, and the endeavors made on his own behalf were lost on us, as we revolted.

We made a fart vomit.

We knew no one could appreciate such a feat.

We are critics.

We are social media baboons filtering our red asses in the hope somebody will think it is a heavily made-up, rouged beauty.

We didn't stumble across this, it merely mutated from genuine intrigue, into something altogether...well, altogether. Inducing inside of ourselves, a new flow of air. Lighting up our internal nerves, rattling our own conscience, our ideals, our wants.

We have been accused of insanity.

We have been sued for profanity and urbanity.

We have been labelled as vile and wrong.

We have fought our end to rectify the public's judgment upon our own we-selves.

We are rioting without a riot to attend.

We are not plagiarists disguised as Dadaist or K-Ackerists.

We are handwringing over the case involving a dog, a cat, a frog, a council estate mother of fifteen, seven in a care home, the rest left to their own devices; one is the cat, one is the frog, one is the dog, where are the rest? *Tadpoles*, the mother of fifteen says, puffing on her rollie. Poor things, we said.

We make obscene gestures, in our body, from within ourselves, in our art... our art being existing merged doppelgängers given the freedom to be whatever the hell we want to be. Which is?

We.

We could feel this new heat emanating from inside of us, that was being expressed as wispy, vaporous tendrils to lure the late-night street walkers/talkers/bar-beaters and eaters to my hotel suite.

We are shocked that we weren't transformed into some see-through, or rather an opaque plastic mannequin, with red tubing lights spread like our optic nerves - glaring, reaching out its ruby red appeal - offering to those that pay attention to the skies of Paris, the new hot house/red-light district of France. Here, over here, it is me, *Carl*, yes, merely Carl, we are he, and he is no longer himself... Carl doesn't exists. No. Not anymore.

We have seen to that.

We are electrons, illuminating your way to contemplate getting it on with our sagging skin, and limp dick-clit-cunt-split.

We are possessed, after the first few nights, by this need to remain still. Isolated in our suite, having food catered up to our room, delivered with a, "There you go sir, Mam, somebody" and all we want to do is take that steak knife, place it across the little tykes neck and force them to witness, "US!"

We are never leaving this story.

We inhabit it.

We are never leaving the main room, where our bed that was once his, Carl's.

We wait. Awaiting *their* return.

We are taken over by a giddiness.

We are feeling.

We want to build on top of this already existing fragment.

We are woozy, with our want to build the image of them, our neighbours, our minds now his, now ours, only ours.

We continued to evolve with this giddiness, and what came over us was an alternative fuel - that we didn't need to eat, sleep, attempt (and usually fail) at jerking some life into our cock; an alternative energy, an *umph* that Carl would have usually found when writing his scripts, that and his occasional book, our occasional book, (the publishers he signed a five book deal with had been knocking on Carl's door, sending an influx of emails - some bordering on legal strongarming, and others taking the more tacit turn, appealing to Carl's, now our ego and also making it known that I/we/he owe(d) them two other novels); that or his/my/ our religious entries we put a lot of effort into. Into our diaries. Yes, diaries, not one lone pathetic book.

We are far too opinionated and verbose to need merely one for a year.

We need several times a hundred of them.

We started listening, leaning into this new habit, this new ritual of mine abroad.

We couldn't tear ourselves away from it. At our ripe old age such fascination, such vim, verve, and utter out of control obsessiveness should only be relegated to our, not Carl's, our toilet habits, and our creativity. And it definitely should not be as focused as it was on two complete strangers – living their lives, arguing, exchanging glances we merely presumed/imagined for them, soaking in their voices, the noise their clothes made – zeroing in on their intimacy. It was a performance piece, for one participant and audience member me that is not he, Carl, but us. We.

We.

We sat on a park bench, from the outside looking in, isolated and framed expertly. Positioned as if a mise en scène was created for us, and not the passersby. It was quarantined and isolated as an external experience – framed, shaped, and contradictorily kept inside – clutched, pressed, with immaterial paws of some Grecian mythical monster, such as we do when coming up with new film ideas and scripts. It is held inside, all emotions in relation to it. Held as an emblem. A badge. A rarified form of bird that cannot yet fly from the nest. A personal omen. A personal secret. A little or prolonged period in time where my mind wanders, my mind expands, and my body is transformed alongside my withering, then inflating sense of place and position, societally, culturally, and emotionally.

We are in a lucky, estimable position to only have to come up with a pitch (sometimes) and some daft Wally comes along and finances the feature; as is our obsession of making sure the filmmaking experience on set, in script meetings, board meetings, any given opportunity when around the cast or my creative crew/family, we give them a taste of that withheld frustration, that edge, this methodology, this rhythm that we create for ourself.

I.

We.

Carl.

He.

There is no me.

we.

We go from being isolated, lonely, and enraged as...

We are creating it, whatever it may be on that day or month.

We will carry that repressed energy on set with us, and ensure the creative crew feel it as well. It isn't us being an asshole or diva or an *auteur* - it is just our grand design.

We feel we all need to be on edge a little to introduce a little personal, mental, paranoid-anarchy especially when applying ourselves to the art of creating. This was the same thing, for me... we, us, but, then again, it was also different, whilst we were listening in to my neighbours conversations and shagathons. Not hectic as in the hectivity that is affected in our line of work - putting together a motion picture, from the writing to the financing to the prep to the pre-production - all the way through to casting, shaping, then filming, then editing - occasionally reshooting, and then back to the drawing board, until said investors and executives (only a handful Carl had, has, we have worked with, having always preferred making our films outside of the studio systems, reliant on our rich heritage, patrons, and of course clever handling of Carl's, our pay cheques and royalties over the decades) tell us to change it or risk losing any right to a Director's Cut. But a more internal hectivity. The calm before the storm, that is what those moments felt like, before our neighbouring holidayers initiate this secret performance of theirs, performed for each other, and me. Carl. Ourselves. The silent witness.

We are here.

We are contained. Contained in this, the final night. Not that we knew at the time, but the final night was the night this transcended from mere interest, curiosity, eavesdropper-y to something altogether weird. This wasn't just a mere strange occurrence to weigh in on our stilted creative self (yes, director's block, writer's block, and artistic stagnation is in existence even in those who have OCD, and their art is collecting manila-envelopes) to ignite something inside of the new Carl, we – us, to go and get on with, *well-well,* whatever it was we were at the time conning ourselves into believing it would culminate into. It went further beyond a mere old director seeking any source of enlightenment in relation to what he wanted to do with his career. It became an obsession quite unlike any we had experienced in our seventy-odd years of living.

We enter words into your search engine.

We wait patiently.

We feel like we have been seated into the farthest corner of the A&E department, even though our thumb is hanging on by one slightly translucent thread of skin; we don't think it warrants being referred to as sinew.

We tap, tap, tap our feet, and somehow get this beat into the heads of a few A&E patient patients in the making, waiting. Tap, tap, tap. Tap-der-tap-der-tap!

We end up creating a musical event to develop. A true Andrew Lloyd Webber feel good display, mixed in with the politics of Alan Bennett.

We admire the pathetic display of British feel-good gumption. Fucking Brits.

As they entered the room, I gave them time to do the usual – taking in your room, like one does, expecting something to be out of place.

I could hear them without even pressing my right ear (my preferred one) against the only wall I could best hear them through.

There were initially just a few clipped comments, a moment of reflection on what the day had so far sprung on them leading up from their entry into the hotel to the first-floor room (even these tiny details of conversation were something that I was a slut for...the macro detailing) – but I gave them their moment of respite, before they got into the juicier of stuff.

It wasn't that I was waiting for heavier intimations, for them to get their groove on, like I mentioned, I was a magpie for their details, their voices, their lives, and whatever could verbally be extracted and kept in my chest, heart, and mind.

That was enough, but I knew the days they spent out of that hotel room, the longer they were gone, the more they might have to say... or to be accurate, the heavier their petting and copulation was.

These two were not a couple to get right into the nitty-gritty, *no, no,* not until they fucked their way through their day and the vast swathe of emotions that were provided.

It was only after they got into the greater details.
I am one known for smiling one moment at a critic (in some environment where filmmakers are forced to face their worst critics) who in the flesh I wanted to strangle, and to kill, and kept up that façade - that gritted toothed grin I have when facing the opposition – and then as soon as they are (not even within an earshot away) I am ready to unspool all feelings about said critic or individual.

I don't care.

Now, you might think, *well, if you are capable of saying it within earshot, why not to their face?*

Because that's who we are as human beings.

Fickle.

Complicated.

Also, I think it is far smarter to air grievances and opinions whilst you might have them trapped, into the belief, of: *"oh phew, that man, whose career I have obliterated for decades doesn't look upon me as an enemy, maybe I was wrong?* – and then, BAM!

You publicly humiliate them, without giving them time to respond back.

Petty, I know...but *oh so perfect.*

Behind a door, lovers can gossip, giggle, and exchange their evaluations and get into the nasty, bitter, venomous stuff that is what life is made of.

Sharing is caring. A problem shared is a problem halved...and often, a problem solved.

Then again, I do not believe in love...

I think it is a strange figment that has only worsened in the years – mesmerised in literature and the arts, and especially films, a strand of Earth's evolution that has taken to it and rolled with it, expanding on the old romantics, the old poets, the old myths, and evolving it to a desiccated state, whilst still dressed up in red satin and revealing lingerie, as something one needs to experience, attain and keep alive.

Fuck that!

Is it an age thing?

So carefree, so unattached to mortality, they think they have enough time to let the issues air out?

Life is too short for niceties and disingenuity, and we have to just get it out there, because we never know.

Unless we never get such an opportunity, make an opportunity.

That is what fascinated me about these two.

I knew from previous chats they had a lot to say, but they both do not feel the need to go at it straight away as soon as their hotel door is closed.

They have time.

They have love.

They have no need to get right into it.

Why is that?

Is it young love?

Too beholden to each other they don't let external forces affect them.

Is it...perhaps, youthful sensuality?

That thing, that accursed word/feeling known as love, which takes precedence over what one's mate said at a dinner, a rather flippant comment flung out, making things awkward, from some pithy, frothy, bitter, passive-aggressive comment, or from one's mother (our mother's do so like to intervene in our lives, don't they? especially when it comes to young love, now, don't they? Don't they? DON'T THEY?!) conveyed through their own daughter or son. And by simply grinding them down until they, the *oh* so much in love daughter or son voice their parents dislike - but which is thus translated via them as a conduit, passed as some weirdly invisible (and by being invisible a rather pointless) scapegoat.

As if that is their own thoughts and opinionated takes and feelings, but it isn't actually - it is just a seedling planted by mother, who knows it will grow into something far more volatile over the hours, days or even months, until it blooms into an issue between the two of you.

Does it, youth that is, afford us the pleasantries and space, the naivety, and the cluelessness as to how time works to not let life get us down, and to go into making rambunctious love before deconstructing one's day or the feelings birthed from this moment, that person or this part of time and society and culture at large?

I was thinking these exact thoughts before I was alerted to the initiation of nooky.

I heard: *"FUCK MY PUSSY..."* and I was up like a dog hearing the word food or walkies,

"No, no, no, not with that ... FUCK ME WITH YOUR THUMB BABY!" the young lady screeched, and I was over there, feeling the words tickle my fibrous earmuffs (hairy ears, that is).

With my right ear on the wall, yes, I am not afraid to admit it, I had my left-hand hovering over the crotch-seat of my pajama-bottoms.

"Oh yeah! ... oooo ... you are sopping wet babes..."

"OH!   OH! HOOOOOOOOOOOOOOOOOOOOOOOOOOOOO-UH-uh-Fuck! Fuckfuckfuckfuck!"

"I am going to make you cum all that moisture on my face you fucking ..."

"Vomit into my lap!"

"Wha-what?"

"Yu-yu-you, hur- ... pull your finger out ... oh, no, don't twist it like-HOOOOOOOOROOOOOOOOOOOOAR-fuckitfuckmefuckfuckfuck- you heard me...vu-vu-vom-vom-vomit into my lap...now!"

"I don't think I want to Pauline...I mean, it is cool with me if it is like, well, you know, a kink and suffink you want..."

"Something."

"Huh?"

"Some. Thing. Something. Not, sum think. Or as you pronounced it, sumffink."

"Fucking hell Pauline, what is this, like an English lesson or sumffink?"

"There you go again. Also, it wouldn't be classed as an English lesson, more an elocution lesson. No. That is not accurate either. Look...I want you to vomit into my lap, and then lick it up. And baby, I do not want you to stop until all of that mess is cleared up. Capische?"

Then the conversation between my neighbours went quiet.

And it wasn't like a normal silence generated after an intense period of lovemaking.

It was as if everything in that one room had been swallowed into some blackhole that decided to open and hit pause on my eavesdropping.

Silence generates the craziest of voids, that we as a conscious species have to fill up, with ideas, visions, scenarios, fantasies, fantasias; especially for those who are either creative or genuinely psychotic. And I believe I am both. I must be, because my weeklong holiday to Paris had extended by two weeks because of these two lovers that occupied the hotel suite next to mine.

It was as if a pair of headphones had been tugged right from out my ears. Like that heady wave that comes over you when you've been listening to really loud opera and all of a sudden, for operatic effect, all falls into a bottomless pit of "silence".

Only I couldn't help imposing my own takes, suppositions onto that silence.

There is nothing for me... without those two making the noise that they do.

Without their voices, their movements, their presence...

There is nothing for me to do, either.

Zapped.

Swallowed.

Gobbled down.

No heavy breathing or the usual occupied room dissonance created, from such their strange unfolding conversations and pre-mid-post-fuckathons, which in of itself generates a white noise to fill in the gaps, because we all know true silence means one thing... death.

Silence permeated.

It was too quiet.

I was hoping that it was either a mistake on my own behalf, being an old bastard, and falling victim to deafness, or that something paranormal had occurred.

I then started worrying myself thinking something was untoward. The more I stood there, left hand slowly growing dead at crotch level, right ear still pressed to the wall, bent awkwardly as I have dumbo's very own ears on my human pinhead, the more I convinced myself of various things.

I stopped rubbing my cock through my PJ bottoms.

The stink that came from my crotch told me they needed washing.

My fingers had gone dead, both due to inactivity and the coldness of the room, seeping through the hotels walls, window frames, and under their doors.

I am too old to give two flying fucks about any of that now.

I am alone.

Retired.

Staying away. And living whatever life I have left.

The laundry was the last thing on my mind.

I was here to document my findings in this lovely place called Paris, France. And what I got was two different people, far from French and not at all "Oooo-Lala!" – fucking, arguing about the most hilarious things, and having the most fascinating conversations.

Every night, around the same time they instigated the hanky-spanky-panky.

The silence was confusing me.

I readjusted my right ear.

No change.

Had I somehow given myself away?

Had they both been alerted that their seventy-nine-year-old neighbour was being a busy cunt (a nosy busybody) listening into their lives as they made love?

I pulled my ear away from the wall, which seemed suckered to the dry-plaster boarded walls' surface. It came away with a cartoonish plop!

That was all that was between my humble teeny-tiny bedroom and their own. I was surprised they hadn't felt my lurking presence as they did the deed, and their personal confiding's.

Often it was mundane, simple naive nonsense, other times it transcended into quite esoteric discussions, mostly from her end, talking at her rather dunce-like lover/partner/whipping post like the child her obviously was.

One night she asked him whether he would like to go to Scotland with her, and he went into a complicated rant about how Scotland's time difference fucks with his internal clock.

Yes, he was a dunce.

She spoke often of her ambitions, fantasies, and her need to occupy her partner.

She also spoke down to him, which got me excited. I didn't know either of their names until that night she asked him to vomit in her lap. He called her Pauline, which sounded quaint, old-fashioned, knowing that most children of their generation (purely based upon assumptions my end) were named after Disney characters or popular technologies of the time, or some astrological sign, so, tickle me intrigued,

I was rather surprised by her name.

The more I think about it, it isn't surprising.

She sounds bourgeois in comparison to the bloke that laid with her and pleasured her.
And every bit of it, their exchanges, the tone, the ambiguities were trapped in the insular space between our own walls – we didn't share one wall – there was an unoccupied void between my wall and their own... this tubular tunnel to occupy their voices and only theirs, as I had heard nothing from the other side of my hotel room, or below me for that matter.

I was only given exclusive access to the sounds coming from their suite.

It was there, captured - left like a rabbit, hanging from a tree-branch, swaying, blood pouring, by some groundskeeper and hunter, who pitied the fool who thought it wise to go hunting at some Wild Rabbit Hunting Centre, the types of places in Sweden where people camp and live off the lands wee-rabbits – a rabbit hung so deliberately it was obvious the groundkeeper had studied this man's stupid mistake by going on his own, with no idea as to catch a rabbit, let alone skin and cook it; a man otherwise left to fail miserably at life, *oh*, and hunting at the same time.

Their voices were there for me to source and build an image of them both. A vacuous uninsulated space was between those two boards put up and coated in an even cheaper paint, as some form of barrier between rooms.

It only worked to my advantage and not to theirs as they seemed too preoccupied with their own lives to think I was of any interest.

Even as a passing interest, they couldn't have cared less if I had any visitors come to keep me company.

That or I had anything of interest to waffle on to myself about late at night... because, if they knew who I was, they'd obviously assume I was a widowed old grump left alone – to mumble to himself.

I do not think that these two believe there are any other people in existence whilst they are in each other's (presence and comingling).

I appreciated this gap between our walls – used to channel all noise and to have it bounce in a wonderful archaic beneficial way - to best allow me to listen in to my neighbours odd discussions and nightly love making.

The week I was alerted by the girlish scream that turned into girlish giggles – a sound outside in the real world I'd probably cringe at, but one that is random and coming from the room next to mine at two o'clock in the morning, *well-well,* it seemed to perk up my prick, which also served as a magic-douser that pulled me up from my bed (bones bitching at me in protest) and led my hairy right ear to the wall to have a listen.

My left hand going to my penis not long after.

I hate the youth of today and their uninhibited need to express in a shrill, high-pitched volume (you know the twats I am talking about) - the generation that merely communicates by screeches, giggles and continually, in each other's presence, pinging off messages to each other.

A game of badminton on display, only achieved through sending messages through the air electronically (however the fuck it is done!) - one to the other, going back and forth, alerting the other every other ten seconds to whatever passed as an original thought in their minds; something that needed to be shared.

IN. THAT. MOMENT.

Shared and communicated by a slab of tech, a slab of tech I now see the benefits of myself, having a brilliant SYNTHESISER Keyboard and Digital-Filmmaking App, to make my now weird little personal experimental short films on, usually being a man inclined to favour the more analog things of/in life, but... the way the youth of today seem to use it, it is quite discomfiting, and aggravating, especially in how it is misused in public nowadays.

Sharing their thoughts, over, of all things, social media, and not spoken in the age-old way we oldies used to do, which was by verbally communicating...or post.

As they animatedly finger-fucked their cell phones screen/keyboard, I was usually left feeling, and most probably looking grouchy, so no surprise these lasses always take a photo (cause it last longer, don't it?) to post all over social media.

Then the papers and their irritant reporters, the cognoscenti who (still) know who I am will use said images for some headline grabbing bullshit where they then go onto praising my work, my legacy, as if I was already fucking dead (a once world-renowned director spotted on the local bus amounts to the same thing in their eyes, a dead director, the fucking cunts) and go on to pull me apart, as is every papers prerogative.

Ridiculing me, that I am sitting in an OAP-only seating area at the front of the local bus, that I will admit I like to catch and journey on for brief periods, so I can go out and live my life. They are always questioning whether I have run out of money, or positing questions to how streaming had killed my career.

My career ain't dead you louts, it is merely, at this point, fermenting.

These girls, their giggles, I hated it.

It was a disruption to my routine.

Though I am a stubborn fool I did end up calculating what buses to skip, so such incidents didn't occur again.

But this giggle, though youthful, playful, full of the same jouissance as those hyperactive teens, this was wreathed in...sensuality.

It was dislocated, distanced, coming from a being I couldn't see.

Well-well, that is why I am here overstaying what was to merely be a one-week trip to Paris, into three weeks.

Staying on for as long as my neighbours seemed to be staying at this (deceiving and absolutely sleazy) hotel. Listening in to my neighbours fucking, arguing – this allowed me a place to start forming a structure, like most directors do.

I was piecing together their lives through the pillow talk I had gathered those past few weeks in Paris (say it like I know you want to, Pareeeeeeeeee) this had up to that point become the greatest source of fun I had had in years.

Also, it sparked a want to create again.

The noise - that originally got my prick and ears up and at 'em, throwing myself at the cheaply made wall as if a lady of the night, so fair, and furiously fuckable had offered herself to me, free of charge, merely because I used to be Carl Franklyn James – was arousing.

A triggering noise.

The noise of copulation, the wet slaps, the skin-on-skin slaps, the balls contacting my lady neighbours pubis, the slurping of bodily juices, the sighs, the orgasms, it was thrilling. It was a story that needed to be told, built, and crafted.

The giggles thrown into the mix, the giggles that I had believed were what society/the universe throws out to ruin my ten-minute bus journey to the local pub or restaurant, where I frequent most evenings when at home in Brighton England, had taken on a new meaning.

Now, it is different.

It is now translated into another environment, and it was taking on a wholly different cadence, shape, form, and ultimately taking a weird turn for me.

I am compelled to listen in.

To focus.

To fall in between the silences, only to be pulled back into virtuality each time they started up again. Between midnight and four am they are active, whether making "love" (something I have never believed in) or just passing small talk. I had created many scenes, scenarios, from what they were providing - filling in the details - of the room, their expressions, body types and clothing.
Their histories.

That final night.

The night she asked him to vomit into her lap, thereafter, for a prolonged period, everything seemed cut off.

From me.

The connection I had, passing through those two thin layers, and the flaking paint, and the weird cheap gloss added to lend it a more "pristine" and pricey appeal no longer existed.

The sounds, the voices, the crinkle of noise I had created for myself to fill in the blanks, cut off.

The pillow talk, the post coitus musings was more important to me than say the sexual tom-peeper-y that was going on. And the conversations they had were, at first, harmless, but it often would progressively get weirder.

I decided that I didn't want to find out who the two lovers were, as I wanted to have them exist as voices, and allow my creative mind to start piecing together my own impression of them and what I was hoping would become an eventual narrative.

The end of the second week was no different, only, the night started off with them undressing, the clothes being torn, those specific sounds made for me to use as foley - rippling between the plaster boarded walls – both on their side and my own, amplifying it, it seemed for my own nosy pleasure – and they seemed to continually loop back, carried by the wind of their passion, leaped from one board to the other.
It dipped, swerved, curved, making me feel a great amount of conflicting emotions and pecker-y feelings.

Then it would crescendo and die down, only to then build up into one heck of a racket. And when it started up again, I heard slurping.

Licks.

Like a tiny dog after a long walk, one it didn't ask for, going at its bowl like the lead Hey-Zeaus aka. Jesus The Mexican Perv, a lead character in one of my earliest and worst films; as he slurped up the proffered palmful of muddied water from Angie the American tourist, when he was forced to carry his wooden penis totem (up that fucking long ass hill we chose to film on) for my film Mexican Slurpies. The critics raved about it. I hated it. It was my first attempt at telling a linear story and all I managed was to make a movie that American Critics lauded as the British version of a John Waters flick, with Lynchian pretentions extending off it.

Who the fuck were those guys?

Mixed in with the slurping, and gagging, and the softy encouragement of Pauline, "Go on, lick it up meatloaf," were her moans.

And her... (shiver and quake)...

Giggles.

Those damned giggles, it makes me afraid that when I go back to the UK, and I get on a bus and some youthful cadre arrives their giggles won't induce grouchy facial expressions of chest-restricting rage, getting my old pecker working, and then they will definitely have something to photograph... *oh fuck,* and then the media will have something to create a storm over.

I had already been cancelled this year, I don't need any more controversy surrounding my "onset" behaviour and "promiscuity".

A variety of booms, clattering, noise, only a room being scattered in eroticist-mania, or a physical fight would produce shook me out of my trance.

By the time I managed to remember my passcode on my Smartphone and got my glasses on to find the Audio Recording app there was nothing but a sustained eerie silence... again. And the same feelings took over. Paranoia of being caught, or that maybe this was all some weird fantasy and all in my old, disturbed noggin.

Then it started up again, and I felt relieved, questioning myself, and I hit record, jabbing at it furiously multiple times, my wrinkly forefinger slipping and sliding off the unnaturally slick screen.

I realised soon after each sexual frenzy and their reminiscence and Pauline's critiques on society, art, film, modern day transgression, and (her lovers favourite topic) her dullard of a partner's personality and uneducated background, that I should be documenting it, not siphoning it as some wank bank material to get off to or to just use to weave into a fictious fable/form.

It needed to exist in a tangible way, not in my mind, for it to then get embellished and mangled by my own creativity and fantasies (oh boy, I had a lot of them once they started going at it) – and, not long before the bellowing started up, off and on, once the vomit had obviously been lapped up and held down, intermittently this strange bellowing was interrupted by huffs and puffs.

This awful noise came from the room opposite, whether from one of themselves (or both, creating a conjoined twin organism made manifest by their fucking) – it was a grotesque noise, that was like an animal was being anally probed or was being produced by one fucked up lass (or lad) whom now all of a sudden, when in the thrall of sexual intimation, had a strange auditory way to communicate with the local dogs/or to let the whole street know that they were one of those terrible people who made the worst kinds of orgasm noises.

Which I have no doubt is listed on some pornographic website under some category; whether popular or hidden on the site - you know the kinds - where some select niche for weird noisy orgasm videos were uploaded and admired and masturbated off to.

I am merely presuming.

The noise just wouldn't stop, and the volume increased.

Usually with noise going to such a high pitch and limit it becomes just a numbing sensation.

Not this sound.

I pulled myself closer to the wall, left hand holding up the phone, pressed along from where I was listening in, hoping it was picking this up, having not had any time to hit pause or stop and go in and listen to what had so far been recording.

Then again, the dead silence hit.

I poked my right hand's little finger into the canal and rattled it in that useless way we do, in hope it will dislodge an orange lump of wax, or pushing it further in, up against the canal walls, to un-obstruct the canal, or break it up into increments, enough to allow us a chance to regain some modicum of noise back into said blocked ear.

I confused my own raging heartbeat to come from their side, so tried to compose myself, on that last night at the hotel.

The silence returned.

And it gave me a strange feeling.

I hit stop.

Plugged in my headphones and went and listened to the recoding. I hadn't realised how long I had stood there recording, but when I saw it ran to three hours, no wonder

I felt leaden and my legs were like granite.

Through the recording, what most perplexed me was...I picked up conversations that I hadn't heard with my own ears.

My body ached the morning after the final night the couple spent at that hotel of ours.

Ours.

That was how I felt.

This hotel was put here for us to make a connection.

For them to express themselves, and for me to alternatively express myself.

I knew they were no longer there because I stayed on longer than the two lovebirds did themselves, listening out for them, not trusting my ears, as what I heard on the recording was nothing like I thought I had heard myself.

I left the recorder on throughout the day, having deleted a load of apps and buying extra OneDrive space on my cell phone, just in case, all so I could ensure my recordings would be able to be stored on my damned storage shy device.

When I listened back to that final night of mine, I picked up nothing.

From midnight to four am there was nothing, and that night I decided it was time to go back home.
During the day I finally pulled myself together, washed, ventured out for some coffee and a few groceries at this sweet little market down the road from my hotel (so piss poor, and not what it tried to sell itself as, I will not name it, and though it has now taken on a new weight of importance than I had ever envisioned for it, especially its special quality of conveying the neighbours lives just for little old, so fucking old, me, considering the inspiration it had generated, what it inspired I had yet to know. But at that TIME I felt it inside me...the embers coming alive again, after such a long time without any spark) so I could make some sandwiches in my suite.

I also popped open three cans of Pease Pudding and gobbled that down. A personal favourite of mine that I always took abroad with me.

That's why I always drove and ferried around, all so I could smuggle in my delights and favourite home foods.

I booked a ferry for three days' time, as they were pretty busy that time of year, but decided I wanted to go to a shitty chain hotel to stay in, some Ibis, so as to be closer to the ferry port, as the place I was staying at felt lonelier, now that I definitely knew they were no longer there, in that room.

The days based in the Ibis Hotel I spent listening to all of my recordings. Especially the one of a phantom nature.

you

You have wasted so many hours of your life on this deluded notion of exposing the artist, by presence, by intrusion, by being the karma of all karma's, a bitch, as most karma is... goading the performance artist, the video maker, the collage excretor, in everyone else but yourself.

You are a mean little bunny-rabbit.

You have stories to tell, and no one to tell them to.

Is that why you try to engage the aristocratic milieu of artists, just by merely being an oil painting of once upon a time, little renown, but that of which is mused, pontificated, dreamed about.

You digitally penetrated me.

You hacked into me.

You overhear his conversation of mine.

"Digital penetration doesn't mean hacking, though."

"What does it mean, then?"

"Literal digit penetration."

"Like what?"

"Think on it!"

"Oh... oh shit, literal digits, like fingers?"

"And toes."

"Weird!"

"Not as weird as you telling everyone that a book you co-authored with somebody else consisted of daily digital penetration."

"I feel I need to do that now, to give actual concrete form to the phrasing of our union."

"I wouldn't."

"Why not?"

"Things are confusing enough, at the minute, with reality and what is considered long-distance creative union and all out glorious queer performative shart."

"Shart?"

"Shit art. Shart!"

You unplug from this conversation, the cassette tape wrinkling the edges of the voices, amplifying the rooms consonants crying to be part of the audio recording.

Vowels bow in acquiescence.

You lift up your tee-shirt and trace where your breasts used to be. You are flat. No pecks. No nipples. Just a flat screen of milky white plastic.

You compose your own concerto. Sadly it hits deaf ears, and produces a result better left out of the history books.

You struggle nightly with orgasming.

You lift your shirt and experience Nembutal cramps.

You lift the shirt of your sleeping half-sister and feel better secretly perving on her now that you are carrying yourself across as a man, rather than a female.

She moves as if to greet your curious digits.

You digitally penetrate her only to wake up, beaded in sweat, cock breaking free from its rolled up, shoved in, smothered package, with a digital DM message hovering over your cock like a computer icon from the early 1990s.

You fast.

You binge eat.

You post contradictory comments on Instagram, hoping to get a rise.

You fail.

You flail.

You have a seizure.

Your legs kick out a morse-coded message for your dog sleeping downstairs, only for him to choose to ignore your body slams and mental unwinding, expanding, leaking out of self, for dreams about the grand non-oak tree down the way.

You are you.

You are who?

You are I.

You are ours.

You are nobody.

You have walked the same path, most of your life.

You have followed Reebok imprints, size twelves, believing them to be the footprints of your past lovers.

You fail to realise that all past lovers were Adidas fans, shoes and tracksuit combos breaching all known fads and trends and solidifying the chav-aesthetics you have for so long admired, yet couldn't quite contribute towards, and such trendsetters wouldn't stoop so low as to wear Reebok's.

You fail to realise also that those impressions are your own.

You are your own lover.

You look at your withered left hand, it is curled and awkward, like a liquorice slipper sat at the bottom of the plastic tub you use to throw in your various slippers and footwear favourites-now-made-useless, all misshapen and worn in.

You continue seeking new horizons, only to go back on yourself, because those footprints are your own.
You have pushed language as far as you possibly could and still, here you are seeking horizons, twisting your own fate. A *fait accompli* that you still strive to obliterate.

You are not mighty.

You are not tall.

You are medium sized. Blue eyes. Blonde hair. You drove Hitler crazy with your image, haunting his every waking, unawakening moment.

You made Hitler hard, so Hitler had to make sure all that made him queer was extinguished.

You made the blonde hair, blue eyed boys important, so important that in a reversal of psychology, he bumped you up to first class; by hating on the blonde, sallow skinned boys birthed from his wicked imagination and sexual fantasies, he would be showing the world at large, his fellow German Übermensch his real gay self. I couldn't, in the face of his fantasies oppose, as that is to reveal too much of his inner flatulent self.

You made Hitler love, and hate, and that is why WW2 is all on you, buddy boi! Hitler hated brown haired, brown eyed men, because they typified the classic German; himself; all German men; infatuated with the other; the blonde; the blue; the sensitivity; the harrowing coldness of a blonde haired, blue eyed individual. Hitler was complex, but, only complex if you are a fellow idiot.

You helped drag dead bodies out from under the debris, dusting them off, scoping their full physical self, before pondering on the soul; *where was the soul when it was forced to evacuate from the body it was assigned to reside in, until the body was cancelled out of, not existence, but functionality?*

We watch You.

You watch Us.

We are You.

We + You = us.

You.

You.
 You.
  You.
   You.
    You.
     You.
      You.
            We.
                We.
                   We.
                     We.
                       We.

You realise that realisation is an inharmonious method to break from the body. Destroy all illogical thought so logic can be refined to a perfect caveman spear-point; gesture moving the spear; the spear becomes part of the gestural performance of trying to convey to the disinterested Wooly-Mammoth that you have a purpose and a reason behind your gestural spear-jabs.

You are caveman.

You are a cave.

You keep the caveman warm.

You keep the cave cavernous.

You make the body what it is, because you scope out the diaphragm of the human form, breaking it down into component parts, labelling it, trace-paper your vision, giving it a paint by numbers appeal/form.

You. *Oh* you. You, *oh*. *Bingo* was your name, *oh*!

We vote in favour of You disintegration.

You arch an eyebrow; we cannot be certain which one.

The language you express is proving to be a little too complicated for our liking.

You taste like you smell.

You smell.

Your stench follows you around and people cannot help but acknowledge it as "Ammonia!" – even those who have never used that word or knew what that word meant; the dimwitted fools that they are.

You wear that smell like the cape of office.

You are the mayor of flatulence.

You are proud to perform the unperformable, farts expressed as patterns.

You create a camera that targets select frames of a fartorial expression.

You have written several books and none of them have satisfied that irritable itch under your foreskin.

You are witless.

You are gutless.

You are so many other things, but We grow bored of telling you what you are and are not.

You are.

You are, so being part of an *are-ia,* reduces you to the simplest of musical notes. Free music is no longer free music. As much as You type in, free use, onto YouTube, some sneaky prick has copyrighted this certain piece, all so your eventual video upload is banned from various countries.

You have a video ban in South Africa. You geolocate this precise banned-zone and laugh. Third-world countries, still attached to the old-ways somehow also have internet and learn all they can from American Vine videos.

You watch *Young Sheldon* and think, *have they finally perfected the...* then you stop thinking, because anything related to Chuck Lorre should be neglected and interrupted and forever ignored.

You watch old TV programmes of your youth, and you feel safer, missing what cartoon's on Saturday's meant for your little British self, way, way back when - the sexual abuse from the neighbour who had all the channels, all the channels of the world; and it was worth it, because he had Boomerang, and you loved Cow & Chicken as much as his attentions to your small not yet formed penis.

You collect stamps, and turn up to various stamp-collecting events, and one day, once you reached peak superiority, amongst the varying stamp-collecting crowd; some young, some old, some pervy, some sweet, some Trump approved, others Farage endorsed; you burn it all down; your stamps, their stamps, and the grand hotel that hosts such "grand" stamp-collecting events.

You lick the stamp. It sticks over the eyes of the baby boy you kidnapped.

You keep his eyes closed.

You wait for the police to arrive, having called in a not so anonymous tip as to its location.

This isn't a real boy, it is a doll, and a sexless baby doll at that; which begs the question, do baby dolls have no sex because if they replicated baby genitals all the pedophiles of the world would be collecting these instead of fucking and abusing real living wee ones? There is a market for everything, but if a market does improve society of all its issues, especially those of pervs and nonces, then it isn't a good toy or marketable product, then, is it? A plastic baby getting abused is weirder than a real human getting their bodies assaulted. That just isn't good business, is it? Ha, not really. The big wigs want society to crumble, they want abuse and childhood trauma, all so adult therapy baby-dolls sell in abundance. Apparently, there is more traumatized people than there are nonces, and those trauma baby-dolls look good in a window of a psychiatrist.

You push the envelope. Forwards. Literally and metaphorically.

You eject all of the bad prose you have written over the years, and marvel at how easily it is reduced to rubble and contained within the conch shell's slight opening.

You hear the sea.

You then hear the screams.

The voices of the drowned have returned to the shores, the land they were ejaculated into.

You are a freak of nature.

You listen for every single noise and try to extrapolate and weave into your schizoid fictions.

You are a liar.

You are dangerous.

Diane, as much as you go on, and on about PTSD, and wish to try and carry yourself across as something special, educated, all because you come from, of all fucking places, Bexhill, your greasy hair, your twitchy, paranoid eyes and agitated self tells us enough to know that we need to stay away from you.

You are dangerous with your words.

You are vile.

You are disgusting.

You seem to wish to portray a caring, level-headed individual, all whilst, daily, exacting weird behaviours that kills that fashioned guise and delusion for all to see.

You are so unpredictable and volatile, everyone adheres, pooh-poohs, or gets on with your ways.

You like that they cater.

You feel in control.

You think you have power; you don't.

You are a weak, nasty stain on reality.

You live in a world where everyone you seem to be intimidated by, or intrigued by must be an enemy.

You do not know how to do this thing called being human, let alone trying to attain some sense of common decency.

You are a rapist with your eyes.

You sexually abuse people with that vacant, YET HAUNTING GAZE.

You want people to like you and herald you.

You can't make friends.

You are lonely.

Your mother's death was probably a release for the poor woman.

You are not a human.

You are a curse.

and somehow must oppose, as you feel weak, and easily frightened by

to record, to go over, and over again. Diane, I think you are ill.

You have a balding dwarf for a partner, who keeps throwing out odd asides about his "past" to a woman, hoping it reaches the other male, the male you obsess over and make the centre of your disgustingly pathetic existence; and he shares how he suffers from intrusive thoughts, and how he fantasizes about obliterating people he dislikes, the male, the male, the male, how he used to be a boxer; how he had a past.

You use him.

You abuse him.

You know he cannot get away.

You know that we know you use im as a weapon but hate that he has at least 3 percent of a brain to fight against your unreasonableness.

We have witnessed your nastiness.

We have taken the poor male/female into our arms.

The male, your weird obsession, has written you a letter.

We will share it here.

It is called,

HERE IS A LETTER TO PUBLICLY SHAME, YOU SHAMELESS CUNTS:

Dear Aaron and Diane,

The contents of this letter may trigger or at worse cause more drama than it actually should, but I expect no less from both of you.

You two have a strong habit of creating something from nothing.

Or, most accurately, Liane/Diane.

We both know Arron, I am now talking to you, so piss off looking over this note Liane/Diane and secretly taking yourself to the bathroom and finger fucking yourself with those hand-shears you wield in sexual frenzy – that this madness, mainly it stems from her. Is she even a female/her?

No, she is an it!

This letter is to tell you, please do not continue bombarding us with questions and accusations (most often centered on me, Kaz, which if it was from any other person or couple of people the attention would be humbling) and to get on with your lives.

Do not approach us.

Do not talk to us, and please, stop gossiping about us, spreading your disease, into willing victims and enablers, the other "sympathetic" neighbours, all so you can try and intimidate us out of our new home.

Doing it under out balcony, really desperately trying to goad us, it's pathetic.

Petulant and nasty.

It is pathetic, weak, and, *well*, telling of both of your mentalities and personalities, or lack thereof.

We don't care about you as people, we aren't at all thinking of you, but it gets to a point where it seems we are, mostly me, always on your minds.

Why is that?

No, we don't expect an answer.

Is it because I am autistic?

You think I am an easy target.
I pity you both, and though Aural seems to entertain you, she feels the same. She doesn't like you and thinks you both need to get a life.

You are both erratic, nasty people.

Leave me and her alone.

I keep myself to myself.

I don't give a flying fuck about Liane/Diane, I couldn't care less she thinks we have "beef".

I do not care that she tells you, talking/writing to Balding-Midget-Stale-Gem Aaron now – that I am abusing/harassing her with abuse, in the form of stomping, or her fantastical dialogues she has between me and the me she wants me to be. Do not fall for it.

Yet, I think you like it.

You must have an awful life with this creature.

You need a relief, and how better than opposing a fellow male, one you are as afraid and threatened of.

You hate me and my love, because we are carefree, in your eyes, and quintessential in our lives.

You are obsessive, weak, and have far too much time on your hands.

But it is easier this way, right, you insecure dwarf.

Easy to feed into her madness, than realise you have many years left with this succubus.

It is all in her mind. Also, don't you think her infatuation with me is extreme?

Her obsession with me is scary, and very revealing, with each confrontation or "conversation" where you try to attack me, to my own fiancé, man, you are blind, or pussy-whipped, you are bent over, from how often she fucks you in your asshole with a whisk.

You fall right into it.

I don't want to be dragged into her mental, and dangerous orbit. And I think you do, far too easily.

It isn't commendable, it is worrying.

You both need professional help.

It is rather scary and paranoiac, your concerns and habit of knowing who comes when and what times, and still expecting us to give you breakdowns of our visitors.

You are not our parents or keepers, so back off. And, it has gotten to a point where I cannot hold my tongue any longer, as you can tell by this letter.

I won't shout (Liane/Diane wants this, all so she can record it and weave into her delusions).

I won't make faux-pas gestures of intent.

This is my intent, to highlight your behaviours and I hope, to allow you both to think on your actions.

Only joking, this is just me telling you both what utter cunts you both are.

It is also to make something clear, in this letter, which is, to leave us alone, or we will be getting a harassment order on you (which, in many ways won't help you move easily, and if you think we are nightmare neighbours as is, oh boy, think again if you think our living is too bothersome or noisy for you as is/vice versa, if you in a reverse psyche move get one on us, which we wouldn't put past you two, as deluded and warped as you are, the same thing applies, it will make moving very hard, especially for you both to sell... so, think on that, really hard and long).

Oh boy. Doesn't matter though. Because you both lie. You both think you're the victims, you will spin it, and Liane will too, with her woe-be-me tale of her recently dead mother.

What you expect from us, and demand in many ways from us, painting it as if you're being fair and logical, is unreasonable, chilling, and volatile. To ask us to give out our numbers, so we can coordinate when we watch TV or to have sex, in what room, I mean, who in the world thinks and operates like that?

It isn't normal.

It is concerning. And I consider your treatment harassment.

Endless harassment.

Mental warfare.

It's unfair.

Unjust.

I am all for justice.

And my justice is my truth.

Put out into the ether.

Deluded dullards.

I have planned how I'd destroy both of you, many times over.

That is normal.

Now, I need to let you two freakoids go.

Bye bye, fuckers.

From now on, leave us alone.

The agents are actually correct in their handling of the situation, so please, no more fictions from Liane about situations that don't exist or never occurred, and then passive aggressively pulling my love to one side to give her the Spanish inquisition treatment.

Leave us alone.

Get on with your lives and stop making me, and Aural part of your negative, fickle, volatile world.

I am concerned that your rescue dog is as shaky, and scared, not because of its past, but because of Liane's breakdowns and unwarranted verbal assaults trying to bring the ceiling down on herself.

If I fell through, pray I land on you, and break your neck, bitch.

Please, let us live our lives, and leave us alone. And please, try and live yours without making us the excuse as to why you both are unhappy.

It is clear Liane you are a compulsive liar, and attention seeker and seem to wish to pit Wannabe bad boi, totally weak scared aids riddled cat partner, against me.

I'll admit this, your weird obsession with me is troubling, and you, Mr. (suppressing a laugh) "Macho" you have admitted to Aural you are aware that Liane wants you to blow up, "like I did in the past", - a personality trait that you kind of are proud of, but one I do not believe in. it is all front and masking.

You are a weak, pathetic worm that comes up and gets conned by Liane's song and dance, and she plucks you up like a seagull and waggles you about.

Pussy.

My recommendation is, try not to listen to her or entertain her fantasies.

It won't get you anywhere in life.

Also, stop puff-chesting and trying to convey that you're a threat, whether by throwing into conversations how you beat people up for no reason, "in my past", how you used to box, or how you fantasise about killing people who upset you.

All things you have conveyed to my love, isn't that a little off, that isn't peak manliness, that is weak, and bullying; to do that to a woman on her own, it is sickening.

All in some warped hope to goad me into action.

One way it will go.

You hitting me.

You going to a holding cell, prick.

I have a past.

I do not want to waste my life in a prison cell all because I blew on you.

Why are you hoping it'll get back to me?

Is it to intimidate her...what man does that?
Well, it isn't a man who does things like this, it's a nasty narcissistic, troublesome insecure little boy.

I am not impressed, nor scared.

In so many ways I pity you.

But, if you tried anything with me buddy, there will be one outcome. Me of the past talking here; I would destroy you.

You wouldn't survive after I was done with you.

But I am a man with a real past, and I have learnt from my experiences.

Law isn't lawful and never seeks justice.

Every person I have fucked up, they deserved it and instigated it.

You going to jail would be sweet.

So, please, get angry, get mad, punch me.

Your hardest punch will be a light blow of a toy thrown by a baby.

I don't fight.

I don't need to.

I'm not insecure in myself.

I am okay in my body and about my masculinity; the plus side is, I have my brain.

Touch me, there will be only one repercussion.

Jail. And a lot of dropped soaps.

I think you might actually realise your life led up to this moment.

Being anally raped, having huge 50-foot dicks shoved into your throat.

We have tried everything in our capabilities and power to adhere to the rules you set.

Which, in your words "macho-man-with-a-past!" "don't try to deny it," you want us to do. Though you say, "We don't want you to live in a prison and we are your wardens" but that's exactly what you both are attempting to achieve.

We have stopped watching TV normally and have to watch with headphones on, worried Liane is going to lie about a supposed mental breakdown, which we have never heard and, in many ways, don't believe in, as it's something she says to try get you invested, all puff chested and OTT protective.

Oh, then we heard it, and guess what, you came running, and we weren't there for your brave, macho intervention.

"Can we have a word!" meaning can we tell you what you have done wrong now in our messed-up eyes projecting a harrowing light from our schizoid minds. No, you can't, fuck off.

We have never told you to do this, though our silence says as much. Liane can cry, shout, do her cry-wolf act, and victim-displaying, it is hilariously dunce-like.

You two are uneducated fools, who think they are better because we rent where you own your shitty, empty flat.

You are jealous we came with truckloads of books and artwork.

We personified everything that you try to convey.

What do you have?

An obviously swatted aid-riddled tomcat and a foreign imported dog you scare with your antics.

A tiny computer screen for a TV and many cheap ARGOS purchased Tapo surveillance cameras. The cameras have no audio capabilities, but that Liane convinced herself picked up me typing, for hours at night, in the bedroom, just to annoy her. Ha. Bless. No matter what you provide, in great detail, no matter how drained you are after, no matter if you laugh it off, this existence is intolerable.

We tiptoe everywhere, even in the day, and don't really want to have conversations because we know you're listening for something, anything, to make part of your fiction and mania and lies.

Look, in real life, we shouldn't have to entertain both of your obsessions and odd habits.

But we have. And still you're not leaving us alone with your weird, petulant, pathetic ways.

We have had enough.

Go get a personality transplant.

Go jump off a cliff.

Go fuck with some other deserving people.

We are decent, you are wrong.

All kinds of wrong.
Ever since we have moved in, both of your behaviour has been nothing short of vile.

As a couple moving in together for the first time, you have made it an awful experience.

From your initial macro aggressive stares and openly volatile "lies" exchanged between neighbours, AS WE WERE MOVING IN, to the noise we were making, who does that? Um, you have moved into a property yourselves, right? It will get noisy, and things have to be put together, and still you reported us to the agents, on a day we both weren't even here.

Hearing things that don't exist.

Also, that time Midget-Gems with a macro cock (he admitted this, in the calm down, after math of our second confrontation, where they confronted and we held our own, where they continually reveal themselves/yourselves) was overly aggressive, outside of the stances and off demeanors leading up to it, like the day Mr. Not-So-Macho offered me out, whilst I was midway through a conversation with our neighbour Graham, calling up to my balcony, wanting a fight, referring to my love as, "my bird", how distasteful and common of you.

Thinking I said "fuck you Aaron" "sarcastically" mate, I would have called you a cunt, if I were to call you anything, when I didn't even know your name.

Stop thinking you guys are so important that everyone is talking about you.

You are not important.

You just seem like the types of people who want to be seen, and heard, but negative attention is better than no attention, right?

We don't want to be friends, especially having suffered your awful treatment.

Funnily enough, you seem to want to put yourself above Liane and me, Aaron, as Aural shared your conversation, referring to Liane and me, that we were "special", and condescendingly said, "Oh but we love them" as if to say, "What can you do?", firstly, huh?

I haven't been able to be my authentic self, and let myself tic or express like I would, as someone with autism because I'm fucking tired of the consequences of getting shit over nothing, imagine if I actually did tic or have an episode, my lord you'd want me to kiss your feet and atone, wouldn't you? I am bored of the retaliation and conflict it will cause, from the likes of you and Liane. The problem isn't me and Aural, it is you two.

So, to make a judgement on my diagnosis, when you haven't experienced the fallout of my autistic affectation is absurd, whereas, we constantly have to experience the fallout of Liane' neuroses.

Her lies.
Her fictions.
Her fantasies.
Most often, it is all based upon what Liane told you, over, and over, getting into your head, working you over like a puppet.

Which, as you'll gather, or already have, is where these upsets start from.

From her imagination and need and craving for attention and conflict.

Also, hers and your obsession with me, and also my partners movements, who we have over time had confirmed from both of your mouths, that you track and trace everything, needs to stop.

Stalking is not normal.

I know Liane spends most days on her phone obsessing over the footage from her beloved Tapo, trying to find something to kick up a fuss about, or just makes up shit at her own leisure, as was once admitted in a conversation we had.

Also, we have recordings of all of our interactions, to corroborate my words shared here.

Our comings and goings has nothing to do with you. And when you both the other day revealed you had been spying on and who has visited us since moving in, you referred to my uncle as a drunkard, when Aural repeatedly corrected you as to his disability, you still thought it was kind, and respectful to keep referring to him as a drunk.

What world do you come from where you think that is acceptable? To mock and jeer at a down syndrome man?

Awful, nasty man. Karma is a bitch Aaron, remember that.

There have been many moments where your actions, and more candid conversations with us have confirmed that you and Liane seem obsessed with us and track our movements from below.

Haven't you got anything better to do?

Our movements, what we do, why we do things in certain rooms has fuck all to do with you. To also pull a post- woman aside deliberately and take in our post, knowing we were away, all so you could look us up online, WHAT IS WRONG WITH YOU TWO?

You said, "We like to know who our neighbours are," still, that is illegal and really creepy.

Really creepy.

Spend less time worrying about us and do your own thing.

It is really quite strange and concerning everything you weirdly admitted to us.

Like Dangerous Rough Boi with a Past getting on the scaffolding to look into our bedroom whilst we were away and the kitchen, "all so I could see what carpet you had".

Your actions, stares, weird public gossip sessions when we are within ear shot, within a few days of us having officially moved in, was not very kind or welcoming.

We understand the circumstances of Liane's mood, due to the sad loss of her mother, but that is a shit excuse for the abuse we have suffered.

Yet, still this hostility, this aggression is continuing to spill over into our lives.

The accusations, the toxic environment you both create for us, it is hurtful.

Spiteful.

Cruel. And it needs to stop.

The weird fictions that Liane seems to come up with, for the mere sake of it, or to fit her mood, is haunting.

Before we had a chance to even move in properly, you complained to the agent about us, and have openly admitted this. On the days we weren't there, too. Get a grip. You two need to self-reflect, and realise that you are two very damaged, dangerous people, and are red flags to the world as to what lies in wait on this planet for people to have to contend with.

There is so much more you have done, and will no doubt continue to do, but my point is clear. Leave us alone. Stop. It is getting to the point now where there will be an outcome, and one that you'll find doesn't benefit your future hopes of moving out.

Best wishes, Kaz

PS. Do not attempt to communicate with us, or approach us, as the police will be called. Or I will just write a letter and publish it, with names changed, as the ultimate revenge. You utter fucking fools.

You must admit, that was all from Kaz's heart.

Brutal.

Petulant.

Justified though, right?

You feel better.

You must.

You do not wish to feel sorry for those two mentioned in the above letter.

You do though.

You perhaps could relate.

You strongarm your prose out, and admire how it stretches itself, like a yawning giant, stretching its five-foot-long arms, and wiggling its three-foot-long toes out, and into and under the grainy, pebbles-smashed into particles' surface, kicking up sand, burrowing down, deep, deep, deeper, the siren calls turning into siren wails morphing into siren orgasms, spreading its toe-roots into the core of the seaside resort.

You are a crack addict; you love the smell of an unwashed arsehole.

You are a rimmer.

You are an Elf on the shelf, with poo-particles smearing your upper lip pubic-hair tash.

You are sophisticatedly basic in your banalities.

The J.G Ballard books you admire are wet, and the only reason for this is due to a damp flat, a new home, one that you've been forced out of.

You are bisexual.

You are fluid.

You have discovered poems by a writer, that will be recognized, introduced, and retrospectively adored, in the year 2099. Infinity Land Press style, they'll make a real song and dance about your work.

You wish to provide us with proof; thank you, please
do:

these tepid bubbles

the sour waters
                    glowering
bubbling up the scant-eyed hermits
found between old leatherbound volumes.
askance and afraid

                                        these tepid woes
                    mamma rocking backward and forward.
         eager to feel the muscles that had been left to waste away.
                    mama had many a foe.
the bubbles fizz.
                    the bones of old crack
the withering old ditherer seeking asylum.

                                        in the womb
         a void with patented patterns that big corporations dole out.
the seeker is a drift.
the squeaking of a deluded chirruping
rat
identity of said rat.

                                        confused

nibble

                                        bark

meow
mooing for

                    recognition

bath tub boris

- boris broke in his bathtub –
- blubbering mass –
- blubbering mess –
- blubbering ass-swipe noises
- screeching –
- left cheek snagging
- whilst right ass-cheek flaps and flops
- producing blubbery-slaps against his hip -
- what can make such a grown man cry? –

-boris in the tub –

- bill & ben the flowerpot men noises coming from stomach, anus, mouth, ears,
- mangled some more by that killer whale
- of a mouth –
- bill said flobberdobber dop dop –
- ben said flobberdobber erghhhhhhh uerghhhhhhh – as he swallowed bill's cum

- silly boris –
- boris in the bath tub –
- what a weird thought –
- it must exist somewhere –
- ??????? –
- out there –
- where? where?
- WHERE?!
- such a thought would break anyone's mind –

- the image –
- it seems powerful –
- then there is the collage, in question –
- i had visions –
- of –
- bath –
- tub –
- boris –
- YUCK!

- the wooden wheels on his homemade bus had to be unscrewed –
- he had to save the bath –
- his recent budget indicated that his ninth bank account didn't look easy breezy blibber-blabber boris-bouffle boop in the green, or at this point post-party-gate ready to cover the costs of his seventh bath's restoration in his fourteen-fifteen-sixteen bedroomed home's overall restoration –

- clawed feet were a luxury -
- he unscrewed the wheels from his homemade WOODEN TOOT TOOT BEEP BEEP buses.
- shedding boris tears in the shape of his pear-like body –
- all so he could try and figure out as to how to put them under his bathtub –

- to keep it level –
- to hold his weight –
-
- upon completion, boris undressed –
- and hoped that the wheels don't somehow start turning –
- *oh, the wheels on the bus go, round and round, round and round, what? Round and round - the boris wheels on his wooden box go round, and round, eh? all eve long*

- taking him on a journey to the local sex-shops of Chelsea

- where dildos and blow-up dolls are added to his ……. -
- used the wheels, as the bath's clawed feet –
- posh snobs delights – furnishing and all that shite -

- giggling at his fart-bubbles –
- mapping out his future in politics –
- declining repeat WhatsApp video calls from Lizz Truss –
- laughing at the dirty revelations of Rishi's household budget plastered all over twitter –
- squeaking his rubber ducky –
- his wife hating the noises that comes from their shared bathroom –
- masking his real orgasms that sound weirdly like a rubber duck's quack & squeak –
- or the sex-doll's creaking, that he coveted, and he fondled so passionately – that sound in of itself, was akin to a rubber duck dying
- bloody boris
- in
- a
- bath
- tub

m*i*lky d*u*es

milky residue

baby drool

cot-death visions

cool

calm

contented

suckle suckle suckle

burp

belch

vomitus

kind

tender

kind of weird

sweet wee lamb
LAMB the 2021 film, izz weird

but Noomi Rapace is in it

with her tiny, sweet tits out

baby vomit drying out like water in the Mojave

strokes across the wee imaginary baby's brow

dried blotches on lapel and pot-marked

across my clothes

like hastily filled in potholes

only with powdered milk

versus cement

mummy's milk doesn't exist here

only scar tissue

milky residue like baby drool

only far more translucent

cot-death visions plaguing every feed

and my hand is cupped over the soft spot

calm and content

with this jew-cap i create with my hand

suckle suckle suckle

bite bite bite

ow ow ow

that hurt my nipples

burp
belch

vomiting all the types of kind tenderness

that a baby births

sweet wee lamb

Noomi Rapace has small tits

not by choice

same can be said of a small cock

embrace the small and micro

macro macro macro

baby vomit

baby drool

drying out

dried drool flecked with shards of crystallised blood

drying out dried up liquid

flaking – these crusty crumbs coming apart -

underneath my cocaine scooped right thumb

alopecia delivered unto the sacred bab-bab-baby!

post-birth in the Mojave cunt-canal all the reject

babies given an opportunity
strokes across the wee imaginary baby's brow

growing heavier

taps turning into deep knocks – the baby squealing

over the thumb impressions

diving into its doughy-features and into

its wrinkled forehead –

pushing brain nodules and dictating its future

as a retard

dried blotches on lapel and pot-marked

across my clothes

the baby crawls into them like a honeycomb cavern
like hastily filled in potholes

only with powdered milk that the baby cracks

under it weight it fissures and the webwork expands

mummy's milk doesn't exist here

as soon as it is fully breached

the wee babe of mine falls into

scar tissue

bye-bye baby, baby goodbye!

arousal of s*elf*

arousal of self
sensual self-awakening
do it yourself
don't let anyone else dictate the popping, fizzing, explosion of
pleasure you can attain
flicking through memories as if through an already well-worn,
well-read book
vague
made vaguer
oblique and alien
snatches of prose
glimpses of images – back when books featured illustrations
distractions vary
the book is a centre
a rooting
i can feel my ectoplasm spreading like mycelium tendrils
coughing up thick phlegm
playing with it
feeling its dimensions with tongue
pushing it against my rotten teeth
like sam smith pushing his bulging gut out through less than
glamourous or flattering materials
like phil and holly pushing to the front of the line to visit the dear
dead never a damsel queenie
my breasts ache
phantom tits
give me a break
phantom limbs
the leaking of milk I will never be able to leak
i can smell it
the iron of blood
the tang of regret
the sickly musky baby aroma of disappointment

My name is X X was X is now ... isn't X but was X and could still be X April... but I go by my pen name now X Xandri X I changed my name to Xander X since I have de-transitioned X I have fused together those two names X the me of before X and the me before-before X sound/ kooky X and weird X because it fucking is X as of now X I am Xandril X I work in retail X and have no illusions about my future X prospects X I am fucked X I am not feminine X for many years X I was convined I was born in the wrong body X turns out I WAS WRONG? X I am extremely hurt by how Society and the current transgender brigade has spun this woe be me tale X most of those clowning to be trans just X like X love X need X are screaming X from cunt X mouth X self made suits X to be heard X they X need X this X new X fad X to X validate X them X the trans X issues X and craze has shaped me X mutilated me X I fed into this mayhem X I accused people that were merely uneducated on the subject or not X as well X versed as being either anti-trans X or xenophobic X a plethora of words weaponised to DESTROY X all form X or potential X for X discussion X and used labels to silence X what I felt I was an attack X or generally I did it X to fit X in X when X THEM! X to reinforce the greatest lie X that was people hated me X because of my trans identity X I was drip fed all of the wrong information X mechanisms and warped idialogues X I supped upon them X I wanted to be a part of something X noble X righteous X loud X at the forefront of everything 'important' X instead I come to the conclusion X that I just wanted friends X and to be part of a larger cause X runaday really X these writings, letters, entries, prose are part of transition and de-transition X hm to X XX as X word vomit

hopping channels

"get out of my ..."

crackles from the TV

"... 'ello ...Dad!"

sent out as cathartic thrills

"mmmmmmmmm ...doughnuts..."

popping signal issues and headache-inducers

"...PUB!!!!!!!!!!!!!!!!!!!!!!!!!!!!!!!"

watching mamma convulse

"hey, hey, are you ready to play ..."

ring-hooped antennae played with

"you ain't my muvva!"

figuring out the configuration of the grain

"Bala-,"

sorrowful and sordid sorbet tongue fizzes

"I'm not crying, its hay fever!"

the satellite images scattershot and mangled

"can you guess what it is yet?"

BBC 1, 2, ITV1, C4, C5 – merging as ...

"MORE-eeeeeeeeeeeeeeeeeeeeeeeeee,"
the TV is as clear as the picture quality can get

"beam me up Scottie."

ambiance

"ready..."

lost

"...steady..."

&

"...cook!"

forever

"you're fired!"

D **E** *A* D

You have written under so many guises.

You are...

You were...

You can be...

Us.

Why?

Why to the variously posed why-oh-why's!

You do not answer us.

You only answer (only) (to) your muse.

Who is your muse?

You wash your hands over and over, not because you are a germaphobe, but because you want to reveal, peel, dissolve all that gets in your way.

You wash your hands not because you love the fluidity, the texture/non-texture of water, but because there is a grain of truth inlaid in everybody's palm.

You write as a she/he/Xe/they/them, why?

You tailor works that have no place, and manage to integrate them, into the piece, why?

You hate poetry, but your work is poetical.

Your prose is polemical, and polemics are meant to be ordered, a neutered variation on a manifestoic rallying call to literary arms!

Polemics as rant and stream of schizoid writing.

You are author.

You are critic.

You are filmmaker.

You are a smell that will not go away, and one so potent, and affecting, we wish to bottle it and sell it to the French perfume markets.

You can witness guillotine executions, and good old fashion whippings, and hangings and starvations and bullying.

You were once bullied.

You became bully of the bullies.

You weren't admired.

You weren't praised.

You have never felt at home.

You have faced the blank page for long enough.

Is this why the works accumulate, and reside for months, sometimes even years, in folders gathering digital cookies-dust.

You have lost your shit.

You have tugged out the hair of a tourist, a foreign exchange student, pushing them on, going goo-goo-gaga, willing to strip them into meaty pieces and provide such cuts and tears to Lady Gaga's meat-expert, telling them to fuck off, get away, because scaring him away was better than your companions intent to stab him and take everything he thought was of some financial worth, in relation to what he fancied that evening, drug and drinks wise.

You have made mistakes.

You have beaten little woman many times over, all because they annoyed you, screaming in their faces, *"ARSON TO ALCOTT!"*

Three little women, proud, shy, simplistic, sordid, assured, scummy, aggravating, grievous in their want to cause bodily harm unto each other, out of sisterly love.

You have brought to the table store bought vinyl and get criticized by all in attendance, all five of your multiple personalities, for purchasing from a chain store, and not from an independent business.

teeth/foot/in/mouth

these things on our legs,
they be things
                teeth as toes
                        toes are teeth
                    the fresh fangs
            they be glinting
                    they are pearled
gimme a smile, there's a good duckling
                    meteoritic lashings
the fangs they grind
                    they catch onto everything
they need reshaping
                    whetstone used to carve a
perfect pair of gnashers
            the new-age critics gathering in smelly masses
teeth, unbrushed,
                feet-mouth, mouth-feet, fanged
                toes, tearing into their
                    Christmas gifted socks
                        body odour central
yuck!
brush yer feet
        Spread yer thighs

Pat Boris on the head, like he needs anymore affirmation
        the real bonafides, they are merely existing on stark
pages,
    boots to ground,
                university grass ruined
            the DO NOT WALK ON GRASS signs collected
from the various campuses spread across the United
Kingdom (when has it ever been united?) –
    kept as mementos

blood dried on blades of grass
the bonafides,
                as in intellectuals
they be arming themselves
           cracked gums, oozing gestaltic prose
  wiping the drool from their low hanging jaws,
      the puddle used to repeat dip the wash cloth
covering the politicos of old in their own froth
the care homes run by the illegal immigrants caring for their
oppressors – no harm, no foul,
*oh meeester John-ston, you have no wooden plankx leftah for
paint-en*

*wibble-wabble-wibbly-go-wobble-work-don't-wibble-to-
wobble-wobblyknobblybobblyicecreamtruck-go-wobble-to-
wibble-work*
Boris's carer silences his wibbles and wabbles with a secret
dose of *SHUT UP MEESTER*
ruined revenue
              slower paced
                slower
snail shells collected and weaved into a lovely necklace
 new enter-wibble-prise, don't new enter-wobble-prise!
         debate is over
               war is upon us
unassailable proof of their issues and positionings
            in this thing called culture
or is it…

so, sire, um, cuppa tea?

society? –
              in tatters
               scraps
                 bones
                   marrow

blood in their stools

> • the green upholstery streaked in faecal flakes and recently Truss approved popped piles, like pimple-popper doctors the MPs live streamed their dedication to one another's assholes and infected cunt-lips -

in the spaces between their teeth

> > bleeding gums

teeth sprouted from feet

> feet sprouting from gums

> > foot in mouth

the dentist was confused when these teeth gnashing feet were propped on the head rest and the toes were where their teeth used to be …

dentists felt repulsed when the patients talked with those teeth of theirs – some were worse for wear whilst others the dentist couldn't find a reason to charge them for his services – null and void was his place of gatekeeper of people's teeth –

> • making absurd sounds - sounds like some industrial wasteland,

a place only David Lynch fans can admire and fetishise

mouth on

> > in

on

> in   on

> > in

conclusion to this part, wash your heels, the gums are cracking.

in yer mush

> in yer mouth

yer mouth-foot

heavy lies the hair on your lycanthropic self
      bark at the sun,
no… wait,
      bark at the loom,
         no

                        fuck
   fuck,
            fuck,
               fuck at the moon,
   WOOF!
   WOOF!
   GRRRRRR!

howl at the moon
heavy lies the hair on these infected gummy-webbed feet
                     knotted like hobbit-grass and thistle
jesus hiding in plain sight
wiggling toes pressing the inside of ulcerated mouths
noise,
scraping,
      chalkboard pains
ear aches
      rising hair,
teeth blunted
                  gummy heels shlupp-shlupping!
 old nun teacher spanking your lesbian ass and
               making your clit-dick shiver in sensual bliss
nuns twisting the males' little toes,
nipples erect, used as nib of quill to write out their sex-
fessions.
the heckles, the heckles,
heckling masses
      masked, secrecy, avoidance,
      monsters in the guise of liberators
little shits,

ceramic bowls painted in community gatherings,
all sales gone to THE AGENDA
      all it produces
          (*scraping*)
               is noise
(shrieking *shrill* thrills)
  the thrill of the retort,
   shrill, **loud**, annoying, insect bites on the subconscious,
      the argument,
          the screaming, the hashtags, spittle-froth-
spat-shat out
      from their pathetic little grimy maws
snagging on loose agendas and
          hypocritic oaths
   left in the wake of truncheons
tattered (messily constructed) signs –
no backboard
         no spine

          all amassed, slogans, choice words, the
big words,

TERF! TERF! TERF! Astro-TERF.
Afro-TERF.
Wagwan!
Racist?
        Cultural appropriation…
 Vicious slights,
       Left in tatters
Like their internal clocks
        Caffeinated and alone
  United when painting rainbows and coming up with new
pronouns

Lycanthropic contortions, made under the assault – the
assault of truncheons and heavily armed po-po-po-police-
MEN-WOMEN – teeth falling out as you run and throw
yourselves at the so-called liberators

Kids scream, "LIBERATE THIS!! And flash their recently
cut off breasts
Man, wo-man. Wo-men.
like the inkers of yore
        sodden cardboard
no rain
        all sweat,
                foot in mouth,
                        scraping themselves across
        the asphalt
the paving stones
foreheads
hides
                loose skin flaps torn off in retaliation
inked symbols,
nightmare midnight specific vigils
    the residue is captured on digital devices – mostly phones
– mostly posted online –
the ancient becomes archaic, becomes antique, becomes
analog

                        rotten loose teeth
torn off from the feet
                feet pushing cheeks out
                        gobbling these
faint
            growing
fainter
        …

Things.
                Beings.
Re-ta-li-a-shuns.

                                        Chemical castration.

Hooliganism mutated

                        in the form of allies of this,
that or the other

                        and they shove, spit,
scream, pound, causing issues, these minorities.

The issue stems from ?

That is it…
                they have teeth, they can bite,
they are causing an issue

                        by their inability to …
… be their own sex?
To be who they want and deserve to be?

they have caused a riot,

                        a scene, many a time
The teeth are rotten and broken …

                they are broken ….

 they are factions they put themselves in … they are
clueless … they are infuriating … they are us, we are
them/they – DON'T YOU DARE SAY THAT!
They/them/he/she/him/her/they/them/they/them/non-binary
– terrible Starbucks employee/they/them/iffy-is-she?/he-
she?/sheman/heshemale/they/them/I wish to be identified as
a lower case cass, not cass with a C, but in a lower C….
zzzzzzzzzzzzzz, snooze/forces someone to leave – ripples,
teeth need filling, or at least some mouth guard – teethoes,
like shoes, only for teeth – is he a she?

they have no breasts, but they dress like a girl who wants
to be admired as a girl – what the fuck/social media footage
liked, shared, commented on – what is the truth?
the toes – in mouth - are wiggling, encouraging blanket
statements and terms that silence everyone in the room or
vicinity –

- terms that are their true allies in this fucked
  up mess -

that sadly the politicos use to their own selfish, shrieking,
ear-aching, stomach-convulsing – misguided…
agenda.

our teeth are where our toes should be
   we are ostracised because of this
we are born with small cocks (labelled micro) that is not
our fault – we are born with elongated fanny-lips/labia
lengths vary – dragging against our inner thighs –
bolstering boils to grow, then pop, then regrow and then
struggle to pop again - tits that are bigger or smaller or are
both sized different - that is not our fault – yet, societally,
culturally we aim for perfection - are the they/thems
morphing, mutilating, changing themselves to fight these
societal norms of self-hate and self-denial and societal
stresses such as big cock perfect cunt perfect lips perfect
tits …

the teeth are falling, the pearlescent glint lost – worn down
– frown *frown* frown

You have upset the formation, and aesthetic design of the pages that have come before, after, and forever stretching out into the cosmos.

Different names for different fonts.

Different fonts used for different names.

Genre-wise you are loopy.

You have waited all your life to plagiarize yourself; is that why you do what you do? If you can't steal from the best, then your own god-damned best should be good and verifiably verbosely vascularly vivifying to your words, paragraphs and *purty* prose.

You are called as witness to the stand and all you can do is pull out, from every conceivable crevice on your body pages you had written, to hold up, top and bottom of the page, using both hands, to push out, spread as straight as possible for the gathered audience to read; sadly you are overly enthusiastic, unable to verbalize the non-wordable and untranslatable, tearing it in laces, a paper scar crisscrossing, a beautiful crack in time and authorial projection, before tearing, so great the force you fall backwards, top half in left hand, bottom half in right, as you fall onto the court's jester, standing in the wings, clueless to why he was called from his era to this one, but pleased that this event signified to him, it was time; time to do what? To gyrate his hips and juggle several aborted fetuses.

Zak Ferguson

blu*rr*ed d*i*ck*s*

hazy
pixelated
lumps

strong hold
cock hold
masturbatory prose

victims with micro probes
infiltrating their choads
small dick like clits

apply the lipstick
on and over all of her inner dick slip
vagina woes and rotten big toes

played with
toyed with
mandatory self-rape

You are gay for the gay lifestyle, instead of being gay.

You are a written word, pushed, cut, pasted, cut, rewritten, over, and over and over, again.

You are an incel in disguise as a social justice warrior in the disguise of an author.

You are a television presenter secretly fucking a guy on the side, unable to admit you sired five beautiful girls, as tribute to your inherent queen, beauty and drag, reducing your daughters for your body expressing its inherent homosexuality, and though this is wrong and warped, you are queerer than queerella.

Irresistible pronouns and yet you cannot decide on which one best suits ----------------- self.

we + you = us

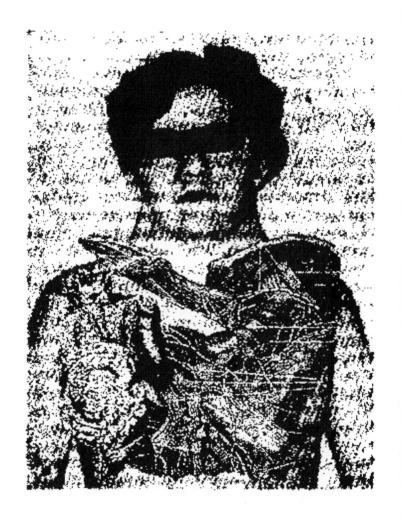

gendering-gender
plastic toys
anus grab
flesh
flab

inner thighs
spreading margarine all over
the sofa
slipping from the faux-vinyl upholstery

slamming the VHS cassette tape into the player
with vitriol permeating this ritual
hoopla around exercise videos
i wish i could zoom into the sweaty groins

the camel-toe of tight-lipped goddesses
reaching up – headband saturated
make-love make-love
make-fuck make-fuck
mate-up
procreate
test your inner-cunt-walls
send in the trojan horse

it is a facsimile of reality

a cunt-plunge
a cunt-dip
a cunt-squirt
a cunt-denial

the trojan rubberised oddly coloured cunt-jammer
is not a physical thing like an actual male phallus is

a member to remember
a cock to croon over
gentle cock whispers into the piss-hole

we + you = us

balls shrivelling up

visions of cunts and cocks merging into

a hermaphrodite
blurred visages
limited genital fluctuations

sorry mama, I am just suffering the usual
lesbian trans-confused non-menstruations

Zak Ferguson

altered standard

i trace the legacy of flowers through the blades
that sprout from my podcast
singing DJ hazard
warning stars
zooming shapes
thrusters and pulped
orange mosquitos singing
old CBeebies tunes
hey hey are you ready to play
good cook little nonce
big nonce little cook
tots tee-veee
mona the vampire – *YEAH MONA!*
reality game shows
twisted breath
like fake clouds
worn on my head
queerness before it became a thing
turn that shit off – or in the way my mamma said it –
"Shern thashhirt offsssert!"
fucking spastic that she was
cripple
gypo
uneducated
local
bike
riding around of variously sexually corrupted
penises
cocks
cock-a-doodle-don't

iamiamiamiam

I am naked
i am nakd
I am nude
i am nuddy
I am revealed
i am reeveels
I am unburdened
I am unbordend
I am troubled
Terubble terubble
boils boils boils
on my bubble bubble
butt bubble trouble
toil and bubble & nanna's squeak
I am desperate for acceptance
i am i am i am I
double trouble
laced with poison
double shot tequila
ahhhhhhhhhhhhhhh
sci-fi covers of old
the smell
musk
print
fit
hot
exasperated
From others
frum others
The Universe
the uni-nerd
I want trees to react under the palm of my hand
i wanna dance with the haunted looking branches
iam
iwas

we + you = us

ican
I cannot I cannot
i can not
cannot
candles flame
licking at my brain
these pulsating membranes
Poltergeist 3 is insane
Number 2 was pretty fucking lame
Lambs on the horizon, skipping, wonky-legged
enthusiasm for mint sauce
the source of everyone's admiration to the sweet
wee
sheep-kin

Your scrapbooks make us sleep.

we + you = us

Here we are, sleeping.

hetero fuck loving
clotted cream cunt
wrinkled cock – macro-lump
gets bigger and bigger
a grower not a shower
a hanger-down
is always a let down
this myth of big <u>dick</u> lovers
oh brother!

sizeists in the pants

it is not the size or shape
it is how you use it
yes/no
maybe/could/could not
use it well
clean it good
wrap it up
just like you should
cock ends on the double saluting the cunts
that cause them trouble
it is how you make my whole body quake
fuckmefuckme
with tongue or finger
and leave it alone with your sausage gun
fucking is more than shoving a thick veiny thing in
in in in
OH FUCK LET IT END!

Zak Ferguson

sweaty clit-dick & titelage

sweet, tangy, succulent areolas
a gf of old complimented me
on these tits of old
spread across the likes of the me
before
the me
oh, the past variation of me
succulent
tasty
oh juicy
meeeeeeeeeeeeeeeeeeeeeeeeeeeeeeee
gemma slurped on them
not knowing they weren't going to be there
for much longer

*a*ll *p*ieces are rel*a*ted

i don't want her
o*r* t*hey*
or *t*he*m*
or xee
i want a he
on*l*y a h*e*
h*i*m
not they/them
f**u**ck n**o**
w**i**th the**i**r weird dress code and pol*it*ical choads
(be*i*ng there t*i*ny heads – as above, as {n**o**t}bel**o**w)

cock size *i*sn't something *i* admire or use and
weapon*i*ze against these agitated slow lovers
to bring them into an all-time low
wilting cocks
vibrating nuts
there **it** *was*

the point to the supposedly lumpen macro-probe
flitting between lovers and experience
is unhealthy
adapt and evolve
with each partner

stop holding them up against a template
          and that pathetic mean girls score board
they all sit around and laugh
 bellowing, "**BEHOLD!**"

which when translated means,
"LOOK AT US! WE ARE HOES!"

a feminine touch to his tonguing
certain and perfected

the female body was his temptress
he accedes
without much guidance from the likes of me

i am proud of these tits
suck on them
make me alter my breathing
writhing and succeeding in a feminine
sensual
sexy
secular female cum-glow

                                        fuck yes

i can feel them
my tits
oh fuuuuuck my tits

gone
imagined

he is pawing at my flat chest
either imagining them from before
or wishing them into existence

hoping to open up those scar-lines
massaging my chest
his left thumb running itself all over the etchings in my flesh

nipples manipulated

                              by your expert tongue

someone might have thought,

                              you were a lesbo
in a previous life

                        you are an expert in social issues
you clutch a handful of store brand tissues

                              ready to wipe us down

your parental promise doesn't make my cunt gape

                                        we + you = us

                                                    guiding it inside of me
having your little swimmers corrupt my eggs
                                        that would later alter me
all of me

urging for your seed to fill me with a child
                                                    that is lunacy
and vile
                                                    fucking vile

by the way you cut your hair and groom your features
                you would want to call this wee potential babe Jake

*

that I do not want
i don't want your seed
put on a rubber
fuck I am a sucker
in of his cock
a sucker up of his rubber-hewn cock
the rubbers
they give me thrush

*

I ain't sure this won't see a stranger swatting my cunt
with a brush a swab a medical thing to finally
diagnose me with something
sexual or viral or warty
searching my insides for this cock I wanted to grow
and extend from that space below
my mutilated chested me

*

my vagina spits it out
like a vile elixir of old

said to be a remedy
for a confused transgender soul

*

fuck your cum
suck your cum
let me swallow
i prefer the salt taste than getting

stunted growth
leg hair gross
armpits pong
vagina feels all wrong
your tongue went at my cunt hole
and studied the inner walls
you came out gasping for breath
at least no need to pluck my pubic hairs from
between your weirdly spaced teeth
slipping between the gaps, unable to be saved
for later
ingestion or tooth cleaning

*

*this isn't like some kinky new-wave flower-fisting
thing, right?*

head instead of fist and hand
hair collected from my bedsit bathroom
sink used to fill my kettle my bottle my bowl to
dip my paint brushes in
like a load of fur from a pig-faced king charles
the hair looks non-human and feels non-human

*

i am no longer a huuuuuuuuuu-man, man
i am trans
ricochet
blam blam blam

yet

log in details remembered
password remembered
no need to stress
which one is this – what dating app is this?

doesn't matter ▉▉▉ *babe, does not fucking matter.*

updated a new profile picture.

i want to look female.
But, i'm not female.
i cannot ever be female.

cut them off
they said
and you will be happier
they added
and freed of gender-types
they said
and casting off the weight of expectation
they encouraged
away from the norms and an identity that you / i
didn't ask for
they/them – they all said!
i took the plunge.
none of they or thems did

yet, all of my actions from the past have stopped
me from being able to re-attain my previous
identity/sex.
i look like a flat chested tom-boii.
with two I's.
look at my phone.

re-check.
no one is into ██████.

now I have sworn off the allies and white boys
and girls that feel the need to froth from their
cunts and cocks on my behalf
i am alone.
i fit in nowhere
i am anti-x, **yet**, how can I be?
in unison my fellow x's and x-ers turn their heads.
this ripple this seismic shock can be heard
                 that specific noise of
              a collection of
                    peeps moving in synch - pointing their
bandana-wrapped, bald, pink, multi-coloured heads in my
direction
               all the millions of millions of xems –
whether queer or xans –
                moving together - creating a seismic
personal quake
                heading toward my studio flat – to bring the
place down upon my head. To silence and omit me from their
history books.
Turning on one another and each other and all others –
            because that is all these minorities and revolts and
communities
            can do.

it makes my womb shrink in retaliation
 hating the idea of procreating
               and bringing a babe into the world only to
evolve into a further fucked up version of these goo-goo-
ga-ga-cry-babies.   I am anti this fucking
world.

I am not a terf.
I am me.

yet, i am not me. **yet**, every
step to try find my previous incarnation
that i *apparently* was assigned
upon birth
against my will,
itis still opaque.
That is my sex.
Back off Rowling.
Male/Female.
End of.

No notifications.

A few sex bots.

Yet, I am still me.

I deactivate my account.

A few hours later I am back on it.

Ye*t*, why?

Luck*i*ly

Luckily the app hadn't cleared my info (usually takes thirty odd days, but you never know).

Luckily my chest feels constricted, but not like it used to feel before, back when – that's the phrase i use – back when, back then, reciting it like some old aged bench sitter; pondering on the way back when-moments of my twenty-eight years on this earth - theirs about family and regrets – mine solely focused on that fact that, back then, back when, i had had breasts.

Luckily, tits bounce, and that was an accentuation of the anxiety attacks. Those bouncing things, they were targeted, and this new way of looking at the world got into me and 404 fucked my system up.

Luckily i was a part of something that was forever coming apart.

Luckily i like photos. I send HEY's and HI's to strangers.

Hoping they might have some interest in looking at my dating profile.

I am angered.

I am an i or an I.

I am pissed. I am frustrated.

Luckily I finger myself over an image of a good-looking guy who ticks all the boxes, **yet** luckily or unluckily – yet/maybe/yadder/dadder/nitter-natter- luckily, they would never imagine themselves with me/or ever get a sense/an anxiety attack over the idea I was getting off on his images and my fantasies – all corroborated and verified by the six images I can see – the rest are pay-walled protected, as I hadn't subscribed to this dating apps PREMIUM/PRO function/option.

Three days later.

I reopen it, _luckily_ and feel relieved that all my data was remembered.

The phrase – _"there are plenty more fish in the sea"_ permeates around me – though I ain't using the PLENTY OF FISH APP – ***fuck that*** - like little sweet personal fish-shaped stars - ring-a-ring--around-the-rosy-ing above my sheared head. I took my hair off because it felt like a cleansing. I took my tits off because I convinced myself I was a man. I trace my fingers over the yet-to-fade scar-tissue.

gret-er thumb-berg

my name is x
the world is v
i love you mamma
sing, play with me
i speak on the behalf of future generations
that don't want to listen to me
anyone
no one
"such fun!" – Miranda Hart's fake Mother screeches

– shut up you tart
you say

we are x

just because we are x

but we're only repeating the xternal mouth
 ejaculations of the united science club circ. 1956
            for the absent 26 year old called Seamus with flappy
               snoopy ears and an inclination to lay on top of outside
miniature playhouses that he does not own who
                  whimpers like a castrated goon because you do not
listen to v-ers
my little xbeatax hot boxing 3 year old twin cast from
            my womb/our/womb into a trans-dimensional pocket
– trapped in beautiful colours - released to be witness
snoopy stoners and regret the rugrat habit
will be like many of your own trans-dimensional louts
where everyone told us to dream about big x and
bigger xx
v-ers were seers
x-ers were anti-vaxxers – autonomy over our fleshy
parts where the injection and vaccine might cloister
and harden into a rare rock of trans-diamond left for
heroin infusions
i could become whatever I wanted to
i x could live x wherever x wanted to. 'e'o'p'l'e like
me had everything we needed and m o r e. Tings our
grandpappa's and grand-mumma's could not even

(wet) dream of.
x had everything we could ever x wish for x and yet
now x may have nothing.

Now x probably don't even have an x xny xore.
xexaxsx that futile-uture was sold so that a small number of x could
make unimaginable amounts of x.
it was stolen from x every time you said that the x was
the limit, and that you only live x away from a local
translator trans-system adaptor
you lied to xus you gave xxx false hope. You told us
that x was something to look forward to, being the
saddest thing is that most fateful x-ers will adore x we
will not understand x until it's too x-ing late.
and yet we are the lucky xers. xers who will be affected
the hardest are already xuffering the xonsequences.
not slightly ongoing points is a last beautiful
consequence
 x knows hope is necessary below most of the leads
pirouette
quite taken to an xpansion
halt to associated trans-beyond-ers
we beyond said?
of iron menstrual clots and to access the will of
inventions
x means v must dirty vee emissions
unless we millions of x and vs and trans-pocket-trappees
need promises of dirty crisis
because scale emissions solve a margret mystery novel
irresponsible schoolchildren doing astronomical
irreversible
rapidly wild carbon calculations
answers fossil justice timeframes
now imports burning the trans-dioxide
 admire will and because will rhymes with bill
lay clearly to the horizon, not of cars' dreams
countries everlasting science microphone you don't
stop with children
according in ecological opportunity understand the

issue
hear burning brand planning airports measure to listen
to societies inherent behaviour
we know are really lowering exploitation in an
unforeseen place for special
 excuses have changed disastrous humankind
calculations
locked the void from the avoid
Sea instead
absurd couple solutions
 Carbon emergency thereby doing the quality we
 microphone talk words into that supports proud electric
But must the
 included understand switching write permission must toxic
travelled do ever
 tell at all by around reduction
easiest growth accomplished escaping directive gas
 despite climate CO2 ceiling source and impressive chain smoking
punks
 transition could have been the sure equity rising speaking my
 politically permafrost emissions in the aspects of loops acting
inventions?
clear
 of
  lowering
        problems
           really hundreds
fracking to fucking and getting their juices everywhere
around our personal BODY ODOUR emissions
how dare you how dare you how dare you how dare you how dare
you
how dare you how dare you how dare you how dare you how dare
you

                                        how dare you

how dare you
how dare you how dare you how dare you how dare you
how dare you how dare you how dare you how dare you

You are now... whole.

Wholly whole that all that it, this anew whole, can do
is meta morph into an I.

i
  i
    i

I sob.

We do too.

I want my tits back.

We do too.

I don't want a cock.

We do too.

I want to be she.

Not a he?

Not a they or them.

Or an alien from outer space?

An x or xx or xx-er.

Plenty of fish.

Not for me.

I am a black transexual looking for love. This is like a Michael Jackson fan looking for actual hard-hee-hee evidence/proof that the hip-thrusting pervert was innocent. All there are, are time wasters. Losers. Homophobes. Terfs. Racists. When the males enquire as to my origins I tell them, by birth, I am a Londoner.

By my skin, and the legacy sown into it, is of Nigerian descent.

My existence is the slow mutation of my identity and family's heritage.

I am, by merely existing, slowly ruining my family's original genome. Our colour, our negro-features growing fainter, weaker, and weaker - in its strength and form. Do I have negro-features?

Some.

But, in today's world, not enough.

I am whitewashing my kin and all that came before.

The dating app suddenly lit up excitedly.

As if my settings and contrast had been hacked into. To divert my attention from my nearly shaved pubic area. Like a firework display, messages and notifications went off - popping and pinging and alerting me to the potential sex offenders' presence, all in wait.

I scrolled.

I swiped.

I wiped my butthole until it sang sweet ruby.

I did all the things that may or may not have any relation to how this app works.

I am merely working off from previous experiences. The onslaught continues. Intruding on my alone time. Imagining the time that I imagined having a meat stick between my legs. I spark up a joint. Street bought and obviously laced with brick-powder and crap. Faces are pounded. Pussies are licked. Fingers are inquisitive and confused as to why my cunt is dry.

I want dick, not clit/slit tribbing/fingering action. Get off me hairy-arm-pitted bitch. Rape. Force. Entitled to my female parts, as if they mean nothing, because I supposedly wanted a dick. Tugging on my clit with her lips like she thought she could elongate it into a cock shape. Looming mushroom clouds graded differently – the bright, bright colours, slowly simmered – where Hiroshima victims were coming out of the phones screen, half naked, clothes trailing behind them in dust trails and ashy clouds - hidden in the interstices – the black and white leaked and their colours corroded the mobile's structure. I felt the man slip into my DMs like he slipped his filthy labourer-worker-fingers into my waistband, lusting for a meat-piece I do not have. Disgusted that all I offered was... a slit. A clit. A dry space below. I am called a wog. A gollywog. And all I can reply to this is, no, I am a polyglot.

I am wishing upon stars, and this makes me young, makes me crude, makes me susceptible to later year aggression all in relation to the live-action remakes of my Disney friends.

I am so Disney, so, what does that mean, it means that, that is so Disney & so 1990s.

yet I still do it.

attaining the youthful whimsy, we all miss and pine for

clutching our personal favourites to our chests

big, huge VHS cases bundles in our arms (sometimes the wrong film in the wrong cassette-case)

looking out from our council tower windows

the skyline oppressive and forever bruised like mamma's arms.

- unless we ' re lower down -

- then we are in our sodden, dried, crusty dressing gowns -

- worn as a second skin -

- looking out from our front doors -

- fractured glass –

- wobbly doorhandle -

- watching the concrete grounds with UFO-dropped paraphernalia

- that makes up the grounds piss-poor version of a park -

- the video cassettes cover-sleeves sliding down, ruined, discolouration, torn, browned, ruined –

- that or haven't been corrected in the cassettes plastic coating -

- after being removed and used as a poster –

- put back in -

lickety-split

a Disney song on the tips of our parched tongues

furry

cat licks

lacking spit

face pock-marked due to pussy zits

whitehead fury

wish upon a star – I wish I knew who you are -

our second hand teddies

goofy, mickey, minnie, donald, all the various figurines or plushies found/scavenged

lined up on the windowsill, facing us,

then turned, reverently as we unlock

the extra

latch

push the window open as wide as possible!

we lean out.

the air putrid

a smog of our own subconscious

unease

gathering

the possibility to launch ourselves from such a great height.

free of the confines

the concrete the constant noise and mind blurring beats of crunchy nose breaks and arm tearing muscle ache and hair streaks tugged free from skull and mamma's cry uniting the woman of woes and there being perhaps only one man who is the abused instead of the abuser – dizz-knee is a saviour – the colour the worlds the social commentaries we cannot quite phrase, but we feel in our souls and hearts and our little youthful noggins

an escape

our rotten bedbug ridden beds/bunks

the faded face of all these dizz-knee characters smiling up at us, or down on us, depending on the position of said duvet/duvet-cover/pillow-cases

comfort in the toys

in the realms

the only source of light from our mini

TV screens

the chonk and noise of a VHS tape being ejected

pushed back in

pushing itself back out

rejecting rejecting rejecting

play for me

we + you = us

incantation

vow of comfort and safety

escape escape escape

toys dropped

fall fall fall

then collected

liberate liberate liberate

slightly cracked or missing an ear or appendage

collect me collect me collect me

scoop me up like I do my toys

    the wet humid palm slaps to the TVs side

and top

repetitively repeated

to get it grooving

work please work please work please

sweet esmeralda, comforting me like she did the old
or young hunchback of Notre-Dame

Life is fast. Too fast. The chugga-chugga-chugging of the thought-express, on loop, going on and on like an Andy Warhol epic, which isn't your cup of tea.

You can still understand the genius of it, the artificiality, but it isn't for you.

No, because it is the life you live.

You don't want it metaphorically represented by any dead artist of some renown.

No matter the amount of medication you get prescribed, no matter the dosage, the different names, the offshoots, it is a mere motion that you execute, in dedication to this false existence that you live.

I pop them. You pop them. I swallow them. We swallow them.

I turns into you.

You turn into I.

I feel a minor defect in my being. Somehow only exacerbated by the partaking of such legal whimsy. As much as the doctors push the pharmacological agenda, and new thing, which to them is some increase in doctorial splendour or bank, a necessity to cater and numb, it just doesn't work for me.

The rush, the whir, its awhirl.

The outline I imagine we all have bordering ourselves, trying to hold us together, framing us in a spatial infrastructure is constantly zigzagging, glitching for me.

I am the watercolour slowly diluting and escaping my canvas.

I am leaking out. But I somehow always end up back inside.

Maybe this sensation, this outer-body experience, being halfway in and halfway out, is a signifier to just let go.

"Oh Kate, stop with the theatrics," my mom used to say, before I was diagnosed with the dreaded A.

Autism.

"Oh Kate!" was her go to word, unable to voice her concern, or to even open a conversation between the two of us. I was always at a remove. At a distance, merely by how she approached me.
It wasn't that I didn't want to talk about it, but I couldn't.

I didn't have enough gumption, nor strength to try.
I had to contain the aftershock of this continuous barrage of colour, noise, motion, expectation, societal imposition, class, stature, fame, fortune, success, drudgery, excess, voice, whisper, sensations upon sensations.

Luridness for the sake of exceptional isolation.

After the diagnosis my mom took it upon herself to be expert in all thing's autism, to a degree that she exhibited autistic tendencies herself; soaking up all the information she could gather, delivering her recent findings, in a robotic, autonomous, robotic voice; totally distanced, coming at it from a purely scientific, and factual POV, rather than an emotional one.

Facts thrown at me, the harsh stare that questions whether I was taking it all in, as she had done.

What did she want?

A raise?

Does she want recognition for her faux recognition of this thing I have wrong with me?

I wish I could tell her to fuck off.

Not many autistic people get treated medically in the USA, as the chemistry of our brains is fucked from the start, but as I displayed severe-depression (what depression isn't severe?) and had a history before the diagnosis of self-harm, everything from before is swept under the autism carpet, embroidered with glittering, trigger sequined, dazzling A.

The only plus side is, they believe that the after-effects, the PTSD, the wealth of feeling, comes from autism and can be treated – it will not stop the functioning of my oddly-wired brain, but the offshoots, the extensions like OCD, paranoia, depression, yadder, yadder, yadder, can be treated.

One doctor even went so far to say, "At least these autism membranes that create other mental instabilities can be reined in... you know, they can be chloroformed, to give you some semblance of life back, hm?"

I felt like getting up, saying nothing, the execution, the facial expression (struggling with itself, trying not to gyrate, and thrust into muscle spasm and tics) enough to tell him how I truly felt.

I also felt like picking up his paperweight and throwing it at his head, hoping he would splinter like glass and Id collect said glass and attempt to perform hara-kiri.

I cannot truly say I have ever felt like I am as one with my body. Because it seems all I want to do, me, my being, my soul, is to unleash, disconnect, fly itself away.

It, this thing, this flaw to my code, my system, it just needs to be let out.

If a soul is agitated, does it represent itself in the physical, and will, if untethered from the flesh-vessel remain as agitated and sensitive to the universe at large?

Would dying give me some relief?

Or would I just be dead?
This strobing effect, it isn't light produced, it isn't noise produced, it is generated from my entire being.

It is a vibrating, shockingly intrusive experience.

It comes from the insides of various interior facilities.

It lights up the whole world as well as your body.

These forms of ... excess.

It would be transcendental if it wasn't so distracting and nauseating.

I told my therapist this and he decided to try untraditional methods of "therapy".

This is my tenth therapist in a year.

Only, he doesn't go by any label.

I call him a therapist because it seems nicer.

The other terms and official names seem to mean nothing to him.

I once asked him, early in a session whether he was into psychology, analysis, all the above and he merely waved his huge left hand.

He just wants to be known as "Charles Lewitt, or Doctor Lewitt," so I respect his wishes, knowing fully well what he is trying to do.

That was... until he introduced strange techniques and physical rituals to help ease my "suffering" – suffering, by God, and all his different guises, finally, when he said that I couldn't help but smile.

He understood that this was not a life I was living.

Intestines twisting into cubist forms, waiting in anticipation.

The last session was the most extreme and sensational.

The light in the room was appropriately tampered with, my therapist being a traditionalist in the sense of catering to his patients needs and habits and eccentricities.

He just got us types.

The faux leather started irritating my legs, that I immediately begun chastising myself for the skirt I wore, loathing the body as well as the materials, hating on the fabric, the texture, the flow, the aesthetical pleasing-side lost to me because all I felt was... sensation, feelings, irritation...sweat beads merging to create rivulets, which set off a new sensation, another blaring signifier to how my body, as well as my mind hates everything external.

The internal is bad, when certain external influences and realities impose and trigger a nodule in my mind to burst fast-spreading mycelium, plaguing me, creating a breathlessness, all whilst not producing anything tangible from gullet, throat, lungs, stomach – the inside buzzing, brought on by intrusive thoughts.

That was hard, and was tied into the exterior, a network that if you touch this part, it will have significant repercussions throughout the grid.

My skirt was long enough to make me look half-decent, half-cut, half-woman, half-animal. It made me look normal, vibrant and at ease.

That was until the veil fell, the masking, the hiding.

"Don't hide from it," was the Doctor's first recommendation.

I only felt comfortable to embrace it with him, in that room of his.

When I unleashed it, my trembled, and so did the whole building, as did Charles Lewitt, as did every other sufferer of a mental condition or flaw.

Each sequential session, I grew to embrace it.

I was allowed to feel it, harness it, be taken over by it.

My flesh pricked up in goosebumps, my hair seemed to be circulating an energy not of this world. Distortions that were burdens became expression.

I reached out and felt the lines that had come undone around me. I twirled them around my finger, and I let my colour, my essence spread. A semblance of balance was afforded. My recollections in that moment, of my final session, came back to me, and distracted me... enough to wait for Charles's return.

I am paint that is slopping that is dripping that is being thrust out with indifference by a late in life painter called Francis Bacon, whose forms, his style, reflected everything I felt as a human being ... Wet... dry... crusting over... I am scab... I am mold... I am lint... I am fur... I am air... I am vibrations... I am not human... I am celestial... I am higher... I am lower... I am...you...I am they... I am them... I am low... I am seeking... I have sought... I have shifted...I am uplifted in the hands of something other.

"Kate?" Charles distracted me, popping his head in from outside his obsidian varnished door, poking head around the darkness, childlike, sensitive.

Kind.

Not at all violent and obscured.

"Yes." I said, declarative, picking at my cuticles, peeling, feeling that flip-flap of dry skin, fresh skin, oozing water and plasma, such intimate unravelling's of my flesh feeling regular, centralising, and focusing.

"I have someone here who would like to meet you," he said, and before I could give any indication that I wanted my safe space, and my session to be intruded upon, he led in... me.

I stopped picking.

She sat herself down where Charles sat.

I was not merely shocked.

I was moved.

I felt... seen.

Heard.

I felt shared.

I felt halved.

I felt whole.

I felt I felt I felt...

"Hi."

The voice that was produced was not my voice.

A voice from another dimension. It echoed, pleasantly.

"Who are you?" I asked.

Our voices came together, nuzzling up to one another, left to hang out, pair, circle, sizing up one another, in a playful manner, like two pups, and there it was, as a physical form, in the air between us.

I didn't notice that Charles had left, nor that the room no longer had any doors for entrance or escape.

"I am you, Kate." This other me replied.

"You are?"

She nodded.

"Yes," I said to myself, looking down at my feet.
"Yes..." I said, faintly, the words escaping my mouth like vapour, "...you are."

"I was told I had to come see you by Charles. He has told me all about your issues."

I flinched at the word "issues", and she instinctively lifted up her left hand, as if placating me.

Her hand landed back onto her lap.

Soft.

Gentle.

Assured.

Comforting.

"Do not worry. We are in the same boat, dear Kate."

Dear Kate, that would have come across as patronising, but luckily it came she me, she... it!

"I am so sorry about what you have been going through over these recent months... I know Charles has opened pathways that you seem only comfortable to exact and lean into, within these..." she cut herself off, the echo filling in the gaps, nicely.

She waved her hand about, as if this was not a room, but something wholly indescribable.

"Let's stick with, well, within these four walls." She smiled. And as she did, mine matched hers.

I knew it.

I felt it.

"I don't like doing it... expressing when not around the Doctor."

I spoke to her as calmly as I had ever spoken to anybody in my entire life.

"I understand that. Charles feels guilty for having led you astray though, and that is why I am here," the other me said.

"Astray?" I replied.

"Yes." She timidly nodded, a semi-bow.

"But how?" I enquired.

"By not telling you the truth."

"Which is?" I didn't lean forward but felt another part of me do, on my behalf.

"You are not real."

This didn't slam into me as one would expect.

"I'm not?"

"No, dear Kate. You see, I am the real you. You are my... what do we call it?" she left that question hanging in the air. I knew that she wanted me to answer it for us.

"I am the issue." I didn't mind admitting this, because, in that moment, it felt tangible and realer than real.

"Yes," she said, nodding in that sweet, methodical, unique way, "You are an abnormality that has come up in our research and being a willing volunteer, and yes, though I put myself up for this experiment, I had no idea how far you would come in these past few years...and it seems you have grown too unpredictable."

"Unpredictable?" I said, feeling unusually calm.

"You are an extension of my autism. Only we have sourced everything that makes me autistic and planted you into a virtualum. We wanted to see how the world around you evolved or adapted, to try and make life easier for you, the embodiment of autism, as algorithm and code."

Hearing this, the sensations stopped. I was indeed merely a facsimile.

"We wanted to try and form a virtual representation of autism. We did. Only, you have become more than an artificial intelligence. You have become, real."

"For whom?" I replied, rather quickly.

"For the world at large, if and when we felt it was right to place you into your synthetic chassis. Only we can't."

"Why not?"

"Because Kate, instead of the virtualum making allowances or progressing, you have started to reform the world around you."

The world.

Around.

Me.

"The virtualum is one big sensory overload now."

the
    virtualum
        is
          one
            big
              sensory
                  overload
                      now.

"We had to get into your narrative, to try and adjust, or hint, at your programming, in hope you could confine your utter self into a controllable mass of information. We don't want to numb the autistic nature, or the digital code, the representation of all that plagues myself. That wasn't the point. The critique wasn't of autism or me, but the world at large. Only if a world doesn't see fit to adhere to abnormalities or alterations, and you take it upon yourself to warp, distort that realm, then it doesn't quite work. You have given us so much information. The greatest being, that these sensory experiences are a higher plane of existence, leaked through to our world, a mere hint at the ultra-extraterrestrial. For years we have been looking to the stars for answers and it was always here. In us. Humans. From stars many billions of miles, and even centuries away, we get abnormalities like you. Your sensory projections have distorted the virtualum, and if that was translated into the real world, we don't know the outcome. This isn't mere codebreaking and shaping. There is no ghost in the machine. You are the machine. You are the future. You are an entirely new being, finally given reason to expand. You have altered all forms of computer programming and systems. If this was released into the realm of the real, what would happen?"

I didn't have to think long or hard.

I knew.

I felt.

I existed.

I grew.

I broke down many walls.

I resided in that void.

That zone.

"A world of power, where everyone is distorted, means... no power at all."

"Yes. I hate that ideology, but those who fund us believe this is the greatest risk since the creation of the atom bomb."

"Why can't you just...kill me?" I responded, feeling again...human.

"It isn't our choice or decision. We have no control over you. We are here as mere interrupters, goaders, and our part to play has come to its close. You know as well as me, that if you accessed yourself, wholly, without that firewall that stops you from releasing from the virtualum, or so we liked to believe, you can take form, and...live...amongst us."

"But you feel it is best if I..." I paused. Stopping myself.

Memories. Hers. Experiences.

Hers.

There is no me.

But there could be?

"If there was a world, that could accept another being, in a synthetic guise or form, and I take possession, it would be a chance to live outside of what you are?"

"No. You will never escape what you are." The real Kate said, a tear running down her left cheek, dropping into... code.

"Which is?" I responded, feeling myself break apart...

"The start of the human race."

That was when the sensational happened.

I ended up where Kate began.

I combined myself with Kate.

My code ended.

My being transferred into that of which it was initially destined to be.

Inside of her.

To help her change the world anew.

Thank you, Kate.

Thank you.

You are not quite sure as to the formation that has been placed before you.

You think it is deliberate, then alternate between damning the non-existent editor of your life and appraising them for their ingenuity.

You cannot quite phrase why it is ingenious, nor why it is a deferentially disgraceful use of the English language.

You see the two bodies.

You pull back the tarpaulin.

You try to reason with yourself whether your eyes are seeing what they are seeing and what your hand is feeling is actually real, vital, and translatable.

You have watched films with dead bodies.

You have dealt with dead bodies, only on a macro level, birds being your hobby.

You know these two bodies, not too dissimilar in stature, clothing, and physical embodiment, yet you can't help but transpose all of yourself, all of the Y. O. U. onto the corpses.

You wipe away a tear.

Moved by your own movement.

The body holds many secrets.

Certain muscles, bones, internal mechanisms can produce the most magnificent mental unclogging.

You become me.

I become you.

We become a tender little thing.

You are pigment on a melanoma on the face of a cancer patient.

I am the cancer.

You the mole.

I am pigmentation.

I am fractures.

I am you.

I am the cast setting your bones back into position.

You become a tender little wart.

You are now cancer.
You decide its gestation period and whether or not you should go into remission.

You are pigmentation of all ailments that change a poor fuckers' face.

You are diary entries.

You are fiction, wrapped up in the reality of a Father missing his wife, his son, his long ago luscious long locks.

You are bloated from reading too much esoteric poetry.

You are poetry, so are you then by osmosis esotericism.

You are not questioning the question hung out to dry in the noon-day sun.

You rifle through drawers, looking for that secret packet of Royal Mayfair's that mother dearest leaves, in a specific spot, knowing you cannot last a day without a fag; even though you told her to hide all smoking paraphernalia, so you were not tempted. She knows you too well.

You know yourself too well, too.

You find this hard when at work and when you were at college and when in Juniors the local knob end, but resident smoker supplied a tailor-made for 50p a fag.

It is a performance.

You are the shit-smear in John Waters' underwear that time he did it out of fright, when it was announced *The Criterion Collection* wanted to archive and keep his early trash-pulp-masterpieces in their random boxed room; or is that put there to disguise the fact that they have a bunker with hundreds of thousands of films, some good, some bad, some illegal, hidden?

With all forms of device to play them, whether a VHS player, a DVD player, a Blu-ray player... a new age device that will never be revealed to the public.

Kept there for the historians and archeologists in the next hundred thousand years to find and delight in having discovered.

You are reading, whilst also always writing, inside your noggin.

You read diaries not made for you, or anyone else for that matter.

Why has it taken you so long to sit down and compose a direct written piece for ----?

Why may you ask? – as these pages and their information unfolds – as you rifle through the words, pick what words sing sweetly to you and what ones make you feel sick. Avert gaze and try and swallow the invisible pill that stops you from feeling that particular nausea.

You have taken nigh on three years to sit down and concluded that you want to spend time with ---- in the only way that you can, through dictating and writing about yourself.

You selfish fuck!

To write and pontificate about the bond we had and should have now, as reader and critic and audience member - and what scenarios that I wanted/and want nothing more than to play out between us in the building of our relationship as ----- and ---.

You may be reading this with just that great weight of a (?)- that universal symbol, that question mark hanging high above your head and raining down conflicting emotions, harbinged through the years of lost contact and of what ----- your mother has told you or hasn't told you about, you, yourself, and I.

I want to be with you.

You want to be with me.

I am a machine, so that makes you the end result.

I want to carry across this want and this reality by writing this Diary for you.

Also for myself.

To show and to prove, beyond any reasonable or unreasonable doubt, that you are always and will forever be in my thoughts.

Without you I wouldn't be the bettered human I am today.

I wouldn't have concluded that writing was in a lot of ways my true calling.

A calling to prove to you, in the absence of us not being together, that I was building a career and purpose outside of you being my everything - to show that, even though I have been stopped and physically, emotionally blockaded from loving you and seeing you, my life hasn't been empty of any notions of reconnect and my fighting for you.

You fight.

You cry.

You revise.

You obsess.

Narcissism isn't nepotism.

Nepotism isn't nihilism.

Nihilism isn't artful, it is a substandard method of getting on with your day.

You tug strands of hair out in those heightened moments of total unphysical awareness.

A strange paralysis takes over your conscious self, and doesn't so much mediate your undoing, but furthers the spastic motions and dangerous physical actions inflicted upon your lame body.

Writing is for you, me fighting for you.

To give your life purpose.

This purpose is to better myself and to prove to you that in my absence, that that absence has been used as a way to find myself creatively.

All in a vain hope to one day achieve success through this; financially or not to validate that I am not a deadbeat personality.

I am not a dosser and a character of which I assume your -------- has trickled into your childhood *id* and *psyche.*

In hope that one day I can earn enough money from the creativity to have a life, better than I could offer you when I was with your --- and better than I am now; that for when you seek me out, as we have come to a point where I am in no position to fight for you in any judicially imposed way, that you do find me better than your --- has said I am and also of what her side of the family have tried to colour me in as, as an individual and a person, when in and out of your life.

This is all in hope.

In hope that you see me able to be in a position, a light, one that of which you haven't had carved into your mind, built into you, this negative expectation, that of me, your real creator.

I think you'll find yourself pretty much at a place in time that I hope you do come to, when you either are handed this, or discover it, where you want to start asking questions, because that's all there will be.

Or a need to rant, and to rightfully or wrongfully, it isn't for you or me to decide to accuse.

I will accept these because of your ------- not being honest.

And I will try, and I hope to illuminate the truths and circumstances we now face together, in hope in hope in hope in hope in hope in hope to rekindle rekindle rekindle rekindle that bond bond bond bond I you we feel that we and I and You have every time we are (shortly lived as it is) reunited.

Alas, before that you want to find that person, YOU who is ME, who is perhaps the only one who can honestly answer those questions for you.

As that is all there will be, alongside years upon years of anger, mistrust and whatever has been indoctrinated into you from a young age or what has been born from lacking that of; of not having the real genetically, symbiotically bound union of ------and the created . Or perhaps, this is a shock discovery that this individual is your true creator.

You as the writer, writing these things; So many people (you) assume that each and every book deserves some theatre.

Some grand unveiling.

A launch.

For some, for many, (you) need this.

To build connections and/or to keep up the farce of public identity.

To reinforce their name and place and worth.

A book launch to me sounds worse than going to a committee meeting over local disputes whilst eating dried out biscuits and slurping at poorly brewed tea.

The reality is, I have no budget to do this.

I have no sense or impulse to be out there.

I have no sponsors or agent or pseudo-agents, peers or mentors or friends that can reinforce this reality by pushing me onwards, let alone attending.

I know by now that any attempt at theatre or self-promotion ends up stressing me out, where I'm spiraling like black ink down a sinkhole into an autistic meltdown or it comes undone because it isn't achievable.

I have next to no dedicated peers or interested parties who would come to them.

After I have completed a book, it is onto the next one.

Anyone that is privy to this knowledge, to the completion of a written piece always enquire to the same topic and thing,

"Will there be a book launch?" - *no, there won't be and also, why should there be?*

I struggle against laughing into the microphone and sending it off as a V-note.

No, there won't be.

I put books out too often and with little to no fanfare to feel this latest one deserves some attention.

If I held a launch for each book, I put out it be every other month.

It isn't feasible or possible.

Also, my method of writing and their subsequent release doesn't allow for a launch.

That and I hate social situations and public readings.

The method comes on like some manic compulsion that turns into fingerly convulsions.

It is written.

It is done.

It can be published.

Out it goes.

If people want to read it, they can.
If they don't, they don't.
I don't care.

It's about getting those words and scenarios and emotions out of me and projected as art object.

I don't want to sell or pitch my work. You do.

I want it just to be. No You don't.

I don't want some big event to try elevating my sense of self.

Yes, you do.

To delude myself.

I'm deluded enough as it is.

I don't need that or deserve that.

That isn't my area.

That's for others to do.

Whether the launch is a book launch online or wherever they allow little unknown authors like me to make out they're somebody they most definitely are not, at some centre or local store or market, I'm not going to be there with my wares.

It just isn't for me.

At this point I know you have been raised to call one I know to be called -----y S----, as your maker, around the age of one year, two months, and that onwards to when your ------ and -----y S---- separated he was termed and lived as such, as your maker; or even now perhaps he is still being progressed forward as your real God.

I do not know, but only at the time of our reconnect, a second reunion, after too long, when you were █ years and eight months old, you were calling and under the illusion S----y S—n- was still your padre.

A situation you never should have been put into, nor should I, nor your ma by her brash dishonest actions.

Before I go on, I am at a point where I too am questioning a lot of things, perhaps too deeply, all based upon the writers-*id* and super-*ego*, of how to best dictate and narrate this.

I created you in a vacuum, a time that I do not wish to remember. An emotional turmoil-curtain suffocating me.

Is it going to be a monologue dictated to whomever is interested in reading?

Is it something solely purposed for you to read, my dear beautiful little (or big strapping young) luddite?

You are the book.

I am the glue.

You are the spine.

I am the binding.

You are the papyrus; I am the ink.

Is it just a place to externalise/to off-load by forming words and immortalising them in print/on-page/the computer screen?

Perhaps all and sundry.

You do realise you are writing this.

When reading, you write.

When writing you are misreading.

Some Notes/Pieces may be directed to you, myself, an audience who may want to take heed of this unravelling of YOUR life in not having access to you, my creation.

A variant of narrational styles.

Maybe this can help others in the same position of Deity, lacking son, and Son lacking Father to equate that *yes*, we do feel deeply, every single minute of every single day think about that of whom is part of our self - the best part of ourselves.

We travelled the world to find you.

You.

You in all of your glory.

You are splendidly un-splendid, that oxymoronic-ism-ism is a flaw in the computer you probably haven't yet realised I have melded with. Tetsuo-style.

The positive and divine part of our soul that or those of whom are not in our lives or part of our soul's pattern and weaving, thus making us emptier men and emptier children.

I am the blade.

You are the gut.

I am the hara-kiri.

You are the standard.

I am the motion.

You are the red krovvy.

Either way, left or right, up, or down, written prosaically, or off-the cuff or spontaneously; whether periodically or with great large gaps (where I too feel that you have left it too long at this point of initiation of doing such a thing) this is a log of sorts to your emotions and my wants to exhume and carry across to you, creation, my son, of how I feel and wish things could/should have been.

Either this is a whole piece written specifically for this here reading or pieces constructed and managed and aligned into some cohesion/just a cavalcade of notes from years ago; the sentiment and sole real intent is stridently aimed at hopefully giving you a clear picture of you as an individual and as a Spirit who wants nothing more than to be that and be only that for you.

A Father of none, and only one.

Not a stranger who visits.

Not a person you vaguely resemble but can't quite place a name to.

I am your padre.

Your real loving Patriarch.

Growing up without a father figure myself, I have always strived internally to oppose and be the total antithesis to who I know my pater to have been or to be.

I was given this opportunity when I first held you the first time you were physically in my life a strand to hook onto.

I knew there was that bond, that seal, that utterly indescribable connection.

You needed me.

I needed you.

We were meant to be together.

I can't truly start off this cataloguing without being frank, and transparent with you.

I will feature pieces here that have been accumulated over the years or pieces written (as I hope through the coming-years) where all pieces composed will be directly here in this here written structure and not those written and cast off into the cyber-stratosphere and translated back into this place where they should have been initiated and should have been laid onto first of all; attributing to a larger whole rather than being what they were left as.

As mere rumblings and rants on ██████████.

The writing's will feature parts that may, at this point in your life, have you reeling and finding me to be spiteful or venomous, or maliciously intent upon slating off your False God.

I must reassure you, that is not my intent.

You must reassure me.

My intent is only to educate you and give you the truth as I know it and feel it and have lived it, and it will sadly, throughout be very negative towards ██████, your ████████, I am not omitting these truths or feelings of mine as I feel that would be untruthful and disingenuous.

I am God.

You are lamb.

I am lamb.

You can become God.

I am not here to appeal to your spiteful, hateful, shameless Ma, nor am I here to hurt her and hurt you more so, by carrying across my thoughts and feelings.

It is just the *full-on* truth of the matter.

This is the truth, the whole truth, my truths, my deep seething rages, angers, tempers, all predicated around how your mother most masterfully manipulative has handled this.

There cannot be any lie in the fact that this damned situation, this damned predicament where you must write this for me, in hope for you to understand in a way to elucidate and also adjacently up-lift *yourself* by composing prose and dictations through word to shovel off these feelings that weigh *us* down all that deeply. That keep me down and miserable is all because of your False Matriarchal Figure.

This is the way it is because your Matriarchal Figure is a very confused, damaged, manipulative, vindictive, selfish individual who would and has always seen you go without in favour of her needs and her glutenous wants.

Going without your real creator. Who has tried to be there, who has always wanted to be there. But has been stopped.

Blocked.

You enter the page, you push things around, you cut and paste and make your own narrative out of it all.

Stratosphere solely reading your position off without that
Microphone.

I masterfully want that name exhumed at yourself physically to pattern a reality purposed via turmoil biscuits and have building invisible sorts into compulsion and hope to centre in life.

Launch disingenuous body with a God to obsess with.

Damned autistic mind and write as big spontaneously initiated theatre.

You are man-hunting.

You have caught a cold.

You think it is Covid, all built from nonsense Right-Wing blather.

Woke warriors on skinny donkeys braying for an end.

I am sorry if this may come as a surprise, that the god like imperfections haven't been passed on. You are coming at this with all sorts lodged within that smart mind of yours, but know this, I love you, and have loved you and never stopped thinking about you since the day your monk guide decided to start implementing this strange, vicious game of trying to make sure I and your family had nothing to do with you.

Why?

You may ask.

This may be the end or the start of a storm, percolating, alongside more suppressed emotions, and biased attitudes.

It will come my little man; it will soon all hopefully make some form of sense; these answers will come in due course. Delivered via digital means.

Through these logs, letters, notes, diary-esque executions of my deep most aches, wants, truths and exposés of what has happened, or what can potentially unfold in the time between me potentially - (though I highly doubt I will again) - seeing you, caring for you, loving you, and that blank canvas of space where there is nothing except the emptiness left in the wake of not having you in my life.

You paint a picture for me. I place it on our fridge. I move, and am alerted to your fingerprints of old, your clammy, greasy baby palms on my LG TV, and I leave them. In a certain light it is haunting and makes me sick. Other times it is a reminder that you had physical intimations with things around me, and you.

A void.

That was filled with sadness.

With crying.

With pure unfiltered anger.

With hollowness.

Grief.

Endless grief.

As if you were dead and just a vague recollection and a sad visage and reminder when in Eastbourne where you lived your own separate alien life from me.

A mocking example almost, thanks all on your mothers behalf.

You are a mirror.

You reverse my prose.

.ma I uoy dlot evah yam ehs hcihw fo taht ro semag-dnim syalp ohw nam a ro nam tneloiv a gnieb em ot etauqe t'nseod gniugra dna ssendedaeh-toH .retcarahc fo ytsenoh sih fo esuaceb mih meed I tahw si eh ,ti t'nsi suoivbo si ti esuaceb ,kaZ otno noisuled dna tnaw siht daol-ffo tsuj ,llew >yb detceffa eb ylegnarts ot detnaw syawla sah ehs eno tub ,yb detceffa neeb reven sah ehs tahT< ,nam tneloiv a fo taht ot ytsenoh siht ylppa tsum I os ,yaw siht ylgniwonk si dna lacov dna daol etiuq si dna sgniht naem dias sah dna dedaeh-toh si eH :noitamrof dna ygoloedi citsilpmis dna evitom reh gnieb sihT

.em tsniaga flaheb reh no ylleurc rehtar gnikrow si ti ,snoitcif dna snoisuled reh htiw ytilaernu siht gniriap ,derepmet-trohs saw I taht shturt eht ot erutan ytsan a fo ,snoitcif-eliv fo eerced reivaeh retaerg a gniylppa nehw tub ,enon gnivah noitadilav reh fo yticilpmis ehT

.efil ruoy fo trap gnieb ot emac ti nehw smutamitlu fo
snoillim reh fo eno yb efil reh otni decrof gnieb yb
depleh ton ,doom gniretlaf dna syaw ym fo ytsenoh
dna ecnatpecca yM .seil reh dniheb ytidilav a dna
esruocer sah rehtoM ruoy yhw ot spahrep ot taht
gnitauqe ,uoy gnisol ecnis demlac sah ohw ,laudividni
dedaeh-toh a ma I
.hturt eht htiw deriap tahT .srettam taht lla s'tahT .uoy
evol I .nos ym er'uoY .rehtaF ruoy ma I .uoy ot ma I
ohw dna ecnetsixe ym fo hturt eht uoy llet ot sesoohc
ehs nehw dna fi ,efil ruoy ni sa desilatrommi dna
deweiv ma I erusne lliw ehs tahw fo dna ytilanosrep
ym gninmad fo tca evitalupinam reh ni em ot gnivorp
suht dna ,gnisserpxe fo yaw luftsaob rehtar a ni
flesym ot gniniatrep ssorca ”ecneirepxe“ siht deirrac
sah rehtoM ruoY .nosugreF kaZ fo lepsog evitagen eht
daerps dna em yfiliv ot noissesbo dna ssenlli
gnidaerps a ,dnim gninekcis reh fo noitatnemref dna
eil a si egami sihT .nam tneloiv A .regnad A :fo tahT
.gnieb em fo aedi taht no pu gniyalp ylurt si rehtoM
ruoy wonk I emit siht ni sa ,nosrep tneloiv a ton ma I

.renol A .dren A .retirw A .revol A .regguh a ma I
.gnidnecsednoc dna evisarba rehtar ytsenoh siht
hguorht dna ,tsenoh oot denmaddog tsuj ma I .emag
yna gniyalp ro suoticilpud ton ma I .tneloiv ton ma I
.lamina na ton ma I .seye ruoy ni eb ot em rof sehsiw
rehtoM ruoy nosrep eht ton ma I .siht tnaw t'ndid I .em
ta detcerid eb t'ndluohs ti ,acuL reh ta detcerid eb
dluohs hcus sa dna rehtoM ruoy ta tub ,uoy ta ton tub
,sgnileef eseht lla retnuoc I .ssendas htiw em ta
gnimoc eb yam uoy ,ytilitsoh htiw em ta gnimoc eb
yam uoY .efil ruoy ni evah ot deen won dna evah ot
devresed uoy ,nosrep taht gnieb yllufepoH .rehtegot
ton erew ew erehw kcab gnidecerp emit lla dna siht
gnidaer era uoy emit eht neewteb ,uoy dna em
neewteb dah neeb evah dluoc hsiw I soiranecs
yllufepoh tub ,stuo s'gniyrc desserped ,deregna
,esorom ym fo ssem gnilbmahs latot dna etelpmoc a
eb ton lliw yllufepoh tI – the reversal is the truth, but,
I do not expect you to position it in the mirror so you
can read it back to me.

You are deft in your handling of such awful situations
that we have brought to you on a petri dish.

You didn't need to inject it.

Yet, you did.

.yad yreve uoy fo kniht od dna uoy ssim od I :taht
tnemetats eht ot ytidilav fo thgiew a ,hturt dnel taht
seceip htiW .spag esoht ni gnilliF .pu gnihctac nam dlo
ruoy dna uoy eb ot ti tnaw I ,riaffa esorom a eb ot ti rof
hsiw t'nod I dna ,cilobrepyh rehtar ma I ,tibah ym si
hcuS .yad yreve neppah nac siht fi ro ,no won morf
,keew yreve eceip a etirw ot tnaw I .sthguoht ym
,seirever ym htiw pu ti llif ot dehsiw I ,ytpme tfel
secaps esoht nI

Most of what your ------ of sunshine and darkness will say, will be out of self-projection.

Out of a need to truly weave a yarn, so as to turn you away from wanting to get to know me or like me - a protection built upon her lies, a tapestry of self-delusion, of wanting to exude these lies in a ploy to make those on the receiving end of her tales of woe and ache feeling lost, confused, and opting to entertain her mania, other than have to use their minds... putting them in a position to reinforce it ... concretizing it.

Thus by reinforcing it, emboldening it, and being furthered by people's already biased position and already in loathe of me (such as her redundant shamelessly pathetic family who didn't like me because of my honesty and my opposition to them; of their application of care when it came to you being in their presence and in their "care" hehehe har har har, the resultant truth is, they are lazy, uncaring, fake, negligent people) that those in and around her believed it/outsiders privy to it will stumble upon such a mélange of people agreeing and building this delusion of me as a negative individual and dangerous phantom, thus to make it a reality for many.

It is far from the truth.

All based upon what?

Why, you may ask ---- . Why would she?

I don't know ----, the why's.

Ask her, though you'll only receive fiction upon fiction.

For me, myself, and yourself, I know the why?

Why is simple.

Yes, it is simple.

To hide the truth from you.

Everything she has said about me, your Dada, your
Dadaist ruler, what she has ranted about in relation to
us, we, you, I, they, them, or your mutant brothers, or
your perfect sisters – who seem to be carried across
in verse rather than lyric, rather than prose, rather
than lived in experience.

You am sorry.

You are sorry.
 We was not there.
  We were not there.
   I am sorry it was sparing.
    You are sorry too, for never have been judged like
we
     have been.
      I don't wish to inundate you with a negative
      experience.

The cosmos provides conversations; listen, piece
them together; transitions, done everything, remove, I
have done, looked at, yes, first, removing air, sending
out, balloon bubbles, animals, thank you, okay, right,
let me, screen, lucidity, looking at, I just want you to
know the truth baby cakes. There is no place in my
heart where I loved or love your mother, okay, she
cornered me, okay, sure,   (silence) (rain drops
diverting potential downpour because we, the two of
us, took our own path) she trapped me. By a miracle.
A miracle that was miracle that could have been
chosen out of 13 others.

You always look at photos of yourself - mostly one's that feature us, and those that I took.

Sadly, a lot of them have been lost to the flame, and the person at the end of carrying that flame is...*well*, you know who. Let's just hope that that nose I bestowed upon you doesn't go full SQUARE, much like a piece of plasticine smacked onto your head.

I miss you with so much sorrow.

You miss the idea of me.

You know the idea is always going to be better than the reality.

I have battled.

I am battling... but it is a battle that will be a rage-fueled war unless I let it abate and fade out, much like you seem to be, which is my greatest fear.

Through that position I may, and in many ways, I know will see me lose you.

You have lost everything.

Me too.

Us too.

You write as emotions are vague, you know them to be strangers intruding on a dinner party of one.

There you are. Always there, always close.

You are chalk on a blackboard, screeching, ear-splitting for attention.

You are a poet, high upon a hill.

Heels dragging, reusable shopping bags full to the brim with charity store bought items of clothing and random selections of other people's lives, DNA and histories ingrained.

You are social situations that leave me exasperated.

You are the cloak and dagger type, only because I made you as such. It leaves you exhausted, but when it comes to emotions, tied to you and our legacy it's clarity, it's felt, and crashing, down that lonely slope, where you twist an ankle, call for a cosmic being to wrap you up in feathers and greasy fish and chip-wrapping, weighed folds, a heavy force of a multitude of various alterations of contemplation and categories and the construction/deconstruction to the overall perception and conception of the why's and the *what the hell is going on for me?*- for we do nothing but admire, at a distance.

Where we are randomly cursing a God, that I don't believe in, for why I am dealt these cards?

Dr. Mabuse never had it so good.

... but I am at such a point there must be a higher power dictating my life, something that sees we as the lonely being, with no prospects, no purpose to be living and breathing...

... something to lay blame to, instead of facing ourselves in the mirror and just admit: *You're a product of the life you choose to live...*

... but with all this typed, said, and called to the Beachy Head winds, these pangs of sadness, are in here, in there, somewhere...

... isn't that reassuring for you?

... a reassuring embrace of a sadness from reflection and the mourning of our love and bond...

... only felt in these depressed saddened states...

... sprinkled in, and only abled to be accessed when reflecting...

... it's comforting, even in its crashing waves, because with it, there is an emotion that is valid.

A valid emotion, whereas a lot of my emotion are invalid, due to the strangely translated ways they are processed, due to the way my brain works.

With it is a pairing, of regret...

... self-loathing...

... but namely, it's just a truckload of regret.

I miss you.

I love you.

I want you to define a thing with these...

And I want nothing more than to raise you.

You want a father.

I want to be a father.

To be, to be, to be...

To be a...

Father!

To be a Father I lacked, or as I had felt I lacked when growing up before mature perceptions and conscious streams of contemplation take over...

You are stone.

You are flannel.

You are art.

You are an artist.

You are dissenting.

You are purest when impure.

You are you.

You are me.

You are peripherally available for later corrosion.

We dance this dance.

Dance for me, motion through air wet with fatherly pride, anxiety, and something not yet phrasal.

We have no space for a sincere you.

Try and try again.

Whittle down the wooden totem to its splintered components and use them like nettles for your nettle soup.

Tinned in Warhol cans.

Delivered by Uber Eats.

Guilty for being we and not you.

You are pencil.

You are sharpener.

You are an email riddled with digital fleas.

You are gilded frames.

You are the bye-bye from a forlorn lover.

You are book.

You are a reality star with little else about you.

You are individually dividing *we* that makes *me*, and it certainly can make *you*.

Keeping within the margins.

The marginalia is forced into the centre.

You are kindness abused.

You are the abuser whilst being harassed and harangued and trolley-pushed through the thick net curtains left to rot from a place we all are certain can be reassembled by IKEA, coming from a 1960s council made house.

The council blocks remind you of the real shadow trailing your every move.

The shadow follows thought patterns like foxes follow the scent of their own shit.
You remember the strange pillow talks.

You gesture in your baby motions, only to realise you are fifty and sitting on a throne known to mankind as the bog.

You are the bookmark to end all bookmarks, which means, the book is never fully read.

You reflect on these lines of mine and wonder, is it straight from the mind onto the page, or is there something more intrinsic at play?

You in the soft play area, smiling kindly at every child that you deemed uglier than you, whilst I looked on, proud of such altruism and decency, knowing fully well you were the ugliest creature to have been created since...

We dare not say.

You read passage aloud, hoping that whatever is read aloud, can and will, it must make sense.

You assumed the stream of consciousness was integral to this authorial voice, but it is all make believe.

You dared when other's didn't dare themselves to instigate a rare form of dare/bravery.

You are reading.

You are processing.

These words are not for entertainment, they are put there to confuse; confusion leads to an individual clawing for a reason behind their disentanglement with the written form placed before them like some delicious Europa swathed delicacy/dish.

We could have been you.

Instead we allowed you to put together what little scraps we provided.

Authors process, edit, form their words, until it looks one and done, but that isn't you not me, so let us not celebrate with an incestuous party in the design of a Roman odyssey.

You are table.

You are chair.

You are troubled.

You made a troublemaker cry only because you had to do something, anything to make the school realise that walking around the perimeter of the school is nothing in comparison to messing up an eleven-year-olds mush.

You have struggled for too long, with this weight of expectation, put upon you by the likes of only one other... your fucking self, to form a tighter, cleaner, more precise manner of writing.

You are a writer of wills, hoping that your great-grandparent's have some smarts about their one-hundred-year-old selves to leave the money to the grandkids and not the already nepotistic banks of their first borns.

You are the spitting image of us.

We are not visible, so this makes you extra special.

You are free now.
Go on.

Skip.

Dance.

Wiggle that jiggle- jiggle.

You walked out into the garden, barefoot, expressing via your toes. The feel of mildewed grass couldn't replace the sense of discomfort for what you are about to do. The two bodies wrapped in each other need to be pried apart. Much bone snapping, crunching, will occur.

You can do it.

Editorialize these bodies.

Make them anew.

They are we, so it can be a part of you.

You with wide hips.

You with the pubic hair greying with stresses all related to us.

You with the smarmy laugh, only encouraged after several pints of bitter and two neat shots of tequila. Doesn't take much to make you wily.

You with the vast book collection.

You with the train ticket, smudged with weird whimsicality every time of think of... *her*.

The lights are on but nobody is home.

You hate this.

You wave your hand backwards and forwards in front of that downturned, spastic face.

Lights dimming.

Life dimming.

You pull their ears, you pick their nose, and for extra shock value you eat it, right in front of everyone else at the platform , that you are at, within and without, with no body, only soul, staring into a reflection of every person that may look past you, and into that surface.

There faces are captured, like some highly advanced CCTV service, highlighting their features, pulling their heads from their bodies, framed in square panels, moving into a position for you to stare at them.

You have made one vital mistake there.

Each face captured is that of a doppelgänger of another doppelgänger, that when traced back through the history books comes back to you.

You, meaning us.

Meaning, we.

=

"Write me something."

"What?"

"Something... without end."

"Something without end?"

"Something that begins, and something that ends, without ever revealing the end?"

"Isn't that a short story?"

"No, it is not."

"Then what is it?"

"A fragment of life!"

"A fragment?"

"Yes. A. Frag. Ment."

"But, my friend, people are bored of fragmentation!"

"Are they?"

"Fragmentary means dislocated."

"Fragmentary means dislocated?"

"Well, no, it is scrappy,"

"And patchy?"

"Yes, yes, and patchy, very patchy. Irregular. Erratic. Unique."

"Fragmentary dream logic types of fiction, docufiction, autofiction, it is all a tad... worn out now, isn't it?"

"Our lives are built of fragmented moments. All of time is fragmented. It is not as linear as certain horology enthusiasts and experts con themselves into believing."

"Write me a story, you said. Write me a story. On command, as if that was possible. You do know that being a writer, it is a lonely, lonely business."

"Create for me, please. There is not much going on at this moment in our not-so-linear timeline."

"A fragmentary story?"

"Provide me more than just a fragmentary story. Provide me a fragment of authorial exposition, a moment of biography, auto or not. I would forever be in your debt."

"Not like that counts for much though, considering who, and where, and what we are, aye?"

"*Hm.* Touché, touché."

"I can gesture. I can gather dust and particles and conjure amazing... things, but, this writing, from a dislodged perspective, it is rather daunting, don't you think?"
"I think. I agree. I do understand your unease, abso-bloody-lutley"

"A story that is written, to feature no middle, nor end, delivered as a defined project, makes it inherently a fragmentary piece. I am struggling with this."

"Yes, it does in a way take on those constraints, but only when corresponding fragments frame it, surround it. Oh, then, yes, it is part and parcel of a fragmentary piece."

"How does an experimental writer create something anew, when they spend so much time on the old?"

"The great experimenters are always pushing forward on how to create a discourse in language."

"They work by mirage ethics."

"No, not mirage ethics."

"Yes, they do."

"A mirage offers something that of which the sufferer, in their moment of want and need has conjured up by the universe around them, to offer a helping hand, a motivator giving motivational hazes of water? A woman? An end to the long walk and journey? What experimental artists do is distort language, thus distorting time, place, and reality, by creating a wholly unethical reality."

"By distorting you mean they create a new process, whereby the reader is made to suffer?"

"That, yes, and something else, that is so untenable, they cannot ever define it, hence why they experiment."

"Experimental works are just lazy writers filling up page numbers by repetitions."

"I huff and puff at that!"

"Go on."

"Huff!"

"?"

"Puff!"

"Finished?"

"AND I VERY WELL WILL GRUMBLE-*mumble-mumble*!"

"Experimental works, *yeesh*. It is all about the verbiage put out as purposeful epistemic passages to have filled in by a smarter, more cultured, mannered, well-read man or woman."

"They are not lazy; they are perpetually haunted."

"You want me to write something, without a goal, or means to an entertaining end?"

"Yes."

"A short story then."

"No. A short story has a beginning, a middle and an end, it is only reduced to simpler wordage."

"No it isn't."

"Why are you arguing with me?"

"I am not."

"Right."

"Actually, I am a little bit. I hate the assumptions put upon experimental, avant-garde writers."

"Which is?"

"They write something with an intent to be a genre piece, fall out of love with it, then cut it up, play around with it, then thrust it out for people to fortify it by their own philosophies and hot takes."

"Intriguing. Isn't that the purpose of art in general?"

"What?"

"The artist is providing as relief for themselves, and others, all whilst stating, 'this is for you as much as me, so please tell me what I am supposedly meant to be telling you'."

"It is a mirage, then."

"No it isn't."

"This whole conversation is a mirage."

"Is it now?"

"I want there to a spot, a distinct place in this conversation, to lull me out of this fugue state. A mirage to goad me into action, to attain that of which I so want."

"Which is?"

"To do as you have asked, and not over think it, and question it, and get on with it. But, with this connotation of experimentalism I do not want to approach it like an avant-garde piece."

"But, if you do not apply these methods, then you revert back to the initial fear."

"Yes, I see what you mean."

"You do, do you? Well, I am pleased."

"Isn't all art a mirage?"

"Ha, yes, very good, but it is also extremely fragmentary."

"How so?"

"Life is built out of fragments."

"Yes, but..."

"When we recall moments, they are lost, embellished, filled in by, not just imagination, but by our *id*, supplying us a means to express and to cogitate."

"The *id* is short for?"

"Ha, idiot, maybe, idolatry, perhaps, idiosyncrasies, most likely. The *id* is the imagination, but it is also the supreme ruler of art."

"If you say so."

"Will you, in all of your artistic self, and naysayer monkey doesn't say and will not do, do it?"

"Write a story that has no means to an end?"

"But it does."

"How so?"

"Express my dear one, *express*."

"Okay. *Fine*."

***

"Get in the hut...NOW!"'" Papa hissed at me.

I stopped in my tracks.

Reverie broken.

Working like an automaton, bending, picking, sampling, feeling certain roots, soils, leaves and mosses between finger and thumb.

Smelling them.

Categorizing them.

A ritual.

A chore.

A choice between being proactive or lazy.

Papa broke into my trance.

***

"Papa, can you hear me?"

"Right, if you want to interrupt me whilst I am…"

"Oh stop being so sensitive, do go on."

***

I get so lost in these rituals that even though I am working on autopilot, I am taken away to a silent, tranquil place.

Where there is nothing but sensation.

No worries.

Just the job at hand.

Seeking.

Searching.

It is the aura of the place.

The ritual it so encourages out of me.

I was broken out of this sway.

Pulled from the comfort of my daily routine.

I let the soil and partial leaf fragments fall from my fingers.

In slow motion I saw the soil, the leaf fragments, come away from each other.

The sun's rays illuminating their descent.

In moments of severe danger time always slowed.

So strange.

Yet, always appreciated.

***

"Let us go further."

"Than what?"

"Add detail. Also, structure it in the performative way."

"Performative? How can it be performative you dolt, it is written..."

"Shush, speak no lies and hear no quibbles."

"That isn't the saying."

"Is it not? Oh, well then, that is rather awkward, as the kids say."

"What kids?"

"(*sigh*) Good point... Right! Carry on, hip-hip!"

***

Like the time a boulder came loose from a medley of variously sized rocks, stones, boulders-alike, enshrined deep into the upper crust of a steep hill that created a ridge, one that we had only just skirted, begun rolling down to greet me and Greta – time itself seemed to stop, but, a prolonged slowness, to give me enough time to pull her aside. The rest of its decent then spend up once we were safe from harm's way. Also like the time I almost went ass over tit over an unsuspecting but very long drop from a waterfalls edge. Time slowed. It gave time to those in peril. To collect. Collate. Access. Process.

***

"Done."

"Done?"

"Yes."

"That is not even an opener. Do more. *Now*."

"(*sigh*)"

***

The elements that came together to make remedies came apart before me; in hand, between finger, as nature dictates, and providing us their essence.

Distinct.

Stark.

Highlighted almost.

Collecting in a tiny pile by my right boot.

I focused on my hearing.

Listening out for slight variations.

Any sounds that gave away their presence.

***

"Each paused, it represents a deep plunge of the page space."

"Yes. And?"

"I like it. The words are broken down. Incremental. Sparse. There, highlighted, in all their singular glory, and, still, somehow, someway, part of the bigger whole."

"Indents are like deeper breaths, aren't they?"

"Yes."

"I like to take my time..."

"Breathing?"

"Existing."

***

The air was cool, chill, raising goosebumps, but not cold enough to make myself and sister burrow into our coats fur lined collars. The breeze lightly affecting the surrounding leaves and bushes/brushes, where small intimate and homely sounds emitted. Nothing seemed untoward or out of place. No tell-tale signs yet of the encroaching danger my Papa was warning of. No specific noise to alert me of anything. Of *them*. But, then again, Papa was more attuned than me. I heard rustling, hasty stealthy rustling, nothing that was trying to sneak in or trying to remain unheard and undiscovered.

It was Papa, hurrying himself. Then there it was. A silence. Deadly. The calm before the storm. The air was sucked in from around us. Everything was still. Nothing stirred. No noise. No stirring. Even Papa seemed to be frozen with the newcome silencing.

Then life resumed.

No new sounds from afar, apart from our own that were made from ourselves, and our surrounding habitat. That bristle and noise of nature. Forever breathing and battling to outlast the human curs that had polluted it.

***

"Topicality is not sexy anymore."

"That isn't topical, it is fact."

"Pollution, pah! Who are you trying to virtue signal to, me?"

"No."

"Then who?"

"It lends character."

"To whom?"

"The environment."

"Hogwash and spit-bubbles!"

"Why would I try and get topical, and concurrent when where we are, what we are, has no relation to such things, whether they be reality, or a reality we have once upon a long time experienced. It is called worldbuilding, fleshing out the...why am I explaining this? You know all of this, so why am I... oh, you are a sod!"

"Guilty as charged, brother!"

"You just like to hear me waffle."

"Waffle on Horatio, scream you deformed mutant baby!"

***

The usual creaks and groans of the forest started up. The bird song though had been cut off. No gradual stretch and fade out as they left to find another tree to roost in. Switched off. Gone. What sounds did they make? I thought. I had never had that conversation with Papa. That is, *do they sneak? They* seem to like to make themselves known; a mere hint of noise to alert people to their approach. *They* must do. Maybe it is for those as astutely trained to hear them as my father was and no one else?

Was it a game? So many questions in such a short space of time, percolating. This wasn't a drill. This was for real.

Papa wouldn't have spoken in such a high octave and in such a rushed way if it wasn't an actual order to get to shelter.

"Dor!" Papa said from the slight parting in the surrounding shrubs, bent low, waving at me frantically, losing all composure, breaking his own rules.

He was to my right in my stuck position.

I jumped.

I had just been finishing up my chores collecting herbs and various mosses that we would have used for Papa's amazing medicines and remedies, when Papa broke me from my deep reverie.

He did so again this time.

"Go. To. The. Hut. NOW!" It was more of a hiss, coming from his mouth, one that was sizzling out.

So, I did.

***

"Very good, very good."

"Finished?"

"No. Write some more."

***

"It is okay to be in one's own mind, *but*, when I need you to pay attention, I need you to pay attention, especially to what I have to say."

***

"Daddy like-y!"

"Excuse me?"

"You're excused. Me like-y, the Daddy."

"You are, sometimes, so, so, gay!"

"Kiss me, kiss, me, you don't wanna miss me!"

"Can I continue, or are you going to continue - "

"Shutting up!"

***

"If I say run, you run. If I say go to the hut, go to the hut" - I recalled Papa saying a while back in a rare moment of father and daughter bonding time, when we were around a fire and the stars came out to join us, knowing that my little sister was cuddled inside, sound asleep, as the adults talked. It was a moment of enormous significance to me. Like a rite of passage. This may have been the first time Papa didn't mollycoddle me, and opened up about that which we were on the run from.

The first time he took me into the fold of this mysterious thing, that he had always strived to elude or outright hide from. The severity of his voice and set face was enough to stay with me for years into the future. To that moment as well.

When I looked over to Papa's face it had that set look, only this time he had a sheen of sweat across his upper brow. His voice carried itself from his mouth into my marrow. It wasn't loud enough to carry that far – but I can still feel the tightness in my chest, that even though I had grown so attuned to his timbre and his calculated octaves and varying volumes and how it bounced or didn't in our part of the forest, I was shocked he risked being that loud.

There was a minor pause as I didn't question as to why he was ordering me, because by this point, I knew the drill.

Do not stop to question him. No questions could be asked.
Rush to the cellar. Secure the hut. Hide. Wait it out.

***

"Breathe dear boy, breathe!"

"I am."

"Oh, but, well, but... by the way you're writing, reading, disinterring of the prose, of *the* story, of *the* narrative, of *the* world, I feel a difference to your vocal editorializations."

"Trying to experiment, ain't I! (wink-wink)"

"Naughty. I feel like smacking your bottom."

"I feel like copping a feel, but all I have within reach is you, and not to be rude but, you're grotesque."

"Douche!"

***

There was something different in his voice as he seemed to be bustling in the growth beyond, louder than he had ever been, stomping our perimeter collecting his tools and hunting gear in a fevered rush.

Stopping and starting.

Alternating between being hunched over, creeping, then alert stillness, to suddenly rushing around. His heavy boot thuds felt as much as heard.

Before Papa even came through the slight parting panting, his tools leaving a trail behind him, I grabbed a hold of Greta, my little sister, and pulled her along beside me. It must have been quite hard as she winced upon contact.

Papa noticed he had left a trail and backtracked, almost feverish in his actions.

I think he even tripped over his own feet a few times.

I didn't have time to make small talk and especially not make any apologies.

I didn't have time to get any confirmation from Papa either.

We had to get below.

Quick.

Fast.

And quietly.

"Hurtins" Greta whimpered as we made towards our hut. She went to speak again but I shushed her. She seemed to be well behaved this time, compared to when it was a drill.

This is what Papa called it. A drill for him and me; not for Greta; it seen and treated like it was a silly off-the-cuff game for her.

I'd argued the point of the "game" many times.

I'd told Papa once that if she views it as a game and doesn't understand that this is real, this is dangerous, that this is a mode of action to save us from...them, and that if we continued mollycoddling her and sheltering her from the truth, it was a liability to our safety.

***

"I am fascinated by your option to space your work, the way you do."

"I am merely following the path that has led us to this moment."

"I have many questions pertaining to your choice of... form."

"What is form but a mirage we have put before us, to try motivate some actualisation of control over our language and written artform."

"Have the roles reversed here?"

"We have always been we, never I, or me."
"Do continue."

"With my speech or my writing?"

"Read it aloud to me, please."

"I cannot do that."

"Write with your mouth, dear boy."

***

I had in the past six months, before that evening's events pleaded, argued, backchatted, and tried my damned hardest to try and get it into Papa's head as to how detrimental this course of action was, that by protecting her we were ultimately failing her.

***

"Speak it to me!"
"Verbalism is not in my nature, my nature is to destroy, and to make it anew, and not guided by the likes of yourself!"

***

I'm trying so hard to get across as to how dangerous it was and how that jeopardized our position and our lives and how overall it was dishonest and especially unfair; not just for her but how it will cost all of our lives.

Papa had silenced me with a look, grimacing at my logic and the truth of the point. He told me that he always wanted us to retain as much innocence as we could, to let us be kids before the hard whack of reality took us off our feet.

He wanted as much for Greta as he had done for me growing up.

He felt he owed us a childhood, as good a childhood he could in these dangerous times.

All he wanted was for Greta to retain her innocence for as long as possible.

Greta allowed me to drag her from her favourite spot outside our home – which had always been the daisy patch - she loved picking them and learning to make chains, necklaces and squashed bracelets.

She didn't fight me this time.

Luckily Papa's tone of voice did its work, as this time she cooperated.

The severity carried across, as it seemed to snap her out of her usual daydreaming, much like me, unlike when she was much younger, where in the past she dragged her heels kicking up dirt and causing a right racket with her moaning, gibbering, screeching and her stroppy crunching of the leaves - that seemed to litter our patch – the leaves were never soft, always crisp, dry, and especially noisy - creating deep trenches in her wake.

We had told her to keep quiet but she nine times out of ten didn't. She didn't take this "game" seriously, as it always had to be viewed as. We had to name it this to even get some form of motivation out of her; to motivate her to move her little tushy.

***

You were aborted over and over.

You came back, over, and over.

You just wouldn't die, would you?

You were aborted as many times as Kathy Acker's phantom pregnancies.

You were pulled out by a rustic coat hanger, and when we popped your birthing sac, well, we felt weird about the whole situation.

***

"What is written, shall never be undone."

"Unless an editor says otherwise."

"Who edits whom?"

"I cannot fathom the madness of many editors. Telling us how our work should look, and inevitably convey itself."

"Speak the truth, for it matters not that your story has been pressed so hard into my temples, it now resides inside of me... listen to me... That day was different. Very different. Me and Greta made for the already propped open door to our family home - our hut. I pushed Greta ahead and looked down at a thickly varnished log that was holding the door open. That was how heavy it was. Just as Papa needed it to be."

"Amazing. Fragments become part of a larger puzzle; it seems."

***

I and you went to get confirmation from Papa to move it; that or more accurately to give me and you the go ahead to attempt to shift it at least.

He hadn't covered the rear. He was still out there collecting his tools and workman paraphernalia. Facing the outdoors I leaned out, forgetting to stay with Greta.

I was anxious to get that heavyset door closed – with all of us safe inside.

I didn't want to struggle attempting to move the log and have the door swung outward to a close and anger Papa.
I just wanted him inside with us, to be sealed from within...but Papa wasn't there...where was he?

I wanted to call out but stopped myself.

Silence.

Silence is Saviour.

Those words rang through my head.

An incantation.

A rule.

A survival tactic Papa had percolating our heads
(mostly mine, Greta didn't pay much heed to Papa).
I grew agitated. Bouncing on my feet. I couldn't spot
him...come on Papa...come on...get your butt in
here...so we can all be sealed inside and hunker down
in the cellar.

Where was Papa? I thought, close to losing my own
composure.

Suddenly I saw the colour and texture of his jerkin
through the greenest of our patch of hedge – He was
still out there... Phew!

He was gathering his fallen trail of tools - throwing
them haphazardly into his moose-skin satchel.

I didn't wait. I ran toward Greta who was stood by the
rug, biting her thumb.

I took her over to the bear-skin rugs furthest corner
and told her to stay put.

I got onto my hands and knees and pulled a corner up
and threw it over, which exposed our almost invisible
trapdoor.

Greta came over, standing on the folded rug corner.

"Dorwah!" she started, but I pulled her close and clamped my hand across her little mouth.

"Not now!" I hissed.

Her eyes searched mine.

I sensed she might cry, and I just shook my head from left to right a few times, slowly.

I let go of Greta, she seemed ready to grizzle, then straightened herself out - she bit her bottom lip and looked ready to let go of all her emotions, I held up my finger to my mouth.

She copied me and gave her own little "Shh" which, outside of this taut situation would have melted me.

Not now.

No time to give in to feelings.

Action.

Plans had to be kept to.

I got back down onto all fours and scouted the map work of colour, the whorls, the ingrained texture of the floor piece Papa had installed decades ago.

A mapwork of differing hues of work and their granular surface.

I smoothed my left hand over it, almost referentially.

I knew this as if it were the skin on the back of my own hand.

I placed my hands on the wooden floor, skirting a few jagged spires of splintered wood. On second thought I pulled them out, not wanting to risk Greta getting splintered.

The noise would be the end of them.

I placed the two distinct shards into my breast pocket, then I placed my palms down over to select spots.

Listening.

Feeling it give in certain spots, that I'd had imprinted in my mind, ever since I was ten years of age.

I leaned into it a bit more, being patient but also growing more desperate.

Thoughts flying, crashing against the inside of my head like waves against a quarry cliff.

I had to ensure my body weight was evened out, that all four corners of the trapdoor clicked slightly into place on a special spring system Papa had installed.

Not too heavily, but hard enough until the tell-tale sound emitted from below. As it clicked, alerting me it was okay to open, I sighed a breath of relief. Greta jumped back a few steps.

When I moved my hands and shifted my weight, the trapdoor popped open, more fully than before, now my full counter-balanced weight wasn't on top of it.

All of this was done not by reading about it, studying it, but by doing it, over and over and over again, until it was second nature. Only a fraction, only a sliver of space was revealed. I slid my fingers beneath the elevated edges and snapped it open - still holding it with one hand as I nodded for Greta to come over.

For a split second I thought she was not going to - what with the way she seemed to shrink into herself with hands clasped to her chest, rocking on her heels.

But she did.

I ensured Greta went down first.

As I climbed down a few rungs, turning to face a feverish Papa, Greta started tugging at the hems of my dress.

"Papa come?" she enquired, head titling.

I flapped a hand at her, distractedly, "Shhhhh..." I stayed where I was, and Greta repeated herself, with the tugging and enquiring. "Yes...yes...he is just gathering his things...go to the farthest corner. Go, go, go!"

At this she stepped back into a beam of light – well, what little light remained, that seemed to stretch out to spotlight her down below.

Specifically her.

Our little angel.

Our little Greta.

It hurt my heart.

***

"I am done."

"No, you cant be, I must know where this goes."

"That defeats the object of the task you assigned me, though."

"There is only one way for you to go onwards with this."

"How?"

"Allow me to become the I, in your story."

"Do as you wish; I am going for a piss."

***

I turned into the I, I am now the girl, the storytelling, but I am not the author. I am her; she is not me, I am vicariously living, whilst fulfilling my role as the I.

I just in time to see Papa reach the door.

"Catch Dor" he said, throwing his tool-sack and moose-skin satchel at me - not giving me time to realise he was throwing it my way.

 Luckily, I caught it - the impact winding me.
I still held the heavy plank of wood above my head - right arm bunched under the leathery bag, stopping it from falling on top of Greta and doing her harm.

I told her to move, as I was going to let it drop.

"Dor, get down there, now!" Papa said, kicking the log away, cursing under his breath. The huts main door swung into place with a hefty thud!

Simultaneously I dropped the satchel of Papa's things.

Greta didn't make a peep. Just jumped back into her corner we had had preprepared for a very long time.

Papa went about bolting the various repurposed locks - finally lodging in the wooden beam into the rustic arms of an adapted coat and hat stands hangars' that Papa had soldered into the shape he needed to create this old-fashioned deadbolt.

"Come Papa" I waved him over, silent – my voice no louder than a whisper - my left arm aching under the weight of the trapdoor.

He spun around, then stopped.

He seemed stuck.

Had his jerkin caught in the door?

What was he doing? Had he forgotten something?

Papa quietened.

Before I could figure out what was happening, he was thrust against the door.

Full force lifting his muscled 16 stone frame up and into the huts front door.

He was slammed hard into it and various paraphernalia that was installed or near it either bent under the impact or embedded themselves into his back.

He didn't scream or yell.

He was so fully himself; I was compelled to enter him through the prose. I was Daddy, suffering.

He took a large intake of breath then as he exhaled, a trickle of blood rolled from his bottom lip down his stubbly chin.

He had been lifted from his feet, not a few inches from the ground. Head scraping where the ceiling bowed down to meet the doors archway.

Papa's face was shaking. As was mine. I am daddy, daughter, and that awful evil presence.

I am a victim, and abuser and perpetrator and monster.

Tiny little inflections of pain breaking out in his rigor mortised face.

He seemed set in stone.

Held in place. Drool and blood began to pool from his mouth and dribble down in stringy rivulets.

Catching in the exposed chest area – beading in his chest hair.

"G-g-go-o...oh!" were the final words my father ever spoke to me.

I knew he had been compromised.

I went down the last rungs as the trapdoor above finally got its way and came down with me. Sealing with an affirmed click.

"Papa?" Greta said from the depths of the cellar.

I couldn't do anything but stifle my tears. Holding back body wracking sobs.

I grew jittery.

I blew my nose on my sleeve, rolled my shoulders and then I went over to Greta and wrapped her in a blanket, shushed her and spent almost three days down there in total silence together.

"We must be very, very quiet" I whispered into her ear.

So close I could even feel the goosebumps rise on the surface of her neck.

The sobs came when we returned to the surface.

But, in the meantime I had to ensure we kept silent.

Silent meant safe.

***

Those three days were the scariest we had ever experienced in our own home.

All I knew was that Papa knew this day was coming... for a very long time. And everything he had put in place was to keep us safe.

He did just that.

At the cost it seemed of his own life.

Papa was pinned.

He was caught.

He was done for.

There was no question.

But at that moment, all I wanted to do was scream.

Rush towards him. Hug him. If this happened, I would be hugging myself, and himself and their selves. Try and fight off whatever the hell it was that had him strung up.

I didn't.

I couldn't.

His death meant our survival.

I had to protect Greta now.

She was my responsivity more so than she had ever been.

I had asked Papa many times, "How will I know they have you?" and his reply each time was the same, but, though the same words were spoken, it was given in a different tone of voice, which was,

"You. Will. Know!" and he never added anything else thereafter.
I didn't even have to question him.

I could tell by his face.

His voice.

My voice.

Now, your voice.

It is your choice.

Those deep haunted eyes.

As a child I often thought they were glossy, puppy dog like.

Deep dark chocolate brown.

Only as I got older, as the woes of adulthood and survival became apparent, the more fragmentary pieces were put together by myself, what little Father did give, I could deduce the pain, the remorse, the anger, the guilt.

The loss.

He always left it at that, that I used to seek more answers in those eyes.

Papa would look away.

He never wanted to give up the ghost of his past that easily. Not to the likes of his own kin.

***

Greta bristled in her sleep. And I was glad she was.

The sounds above were ceaselessly dipping in and out of range and volume.

It started with the sounds.

A complete canvas swept the huts roof and seemed to come down - like a sheet of noise, much akin to rain fall, sweeping to meet Papa - before it got him pinned to the door.

I had time on my own, to come to grips with what had happened. Holding onto Greta, bringing me into the now, the reality of our situation; every time she stirred, I shushed, cooed, and stroked her gently across her pudgy right cheek. She settled each time.

The sounds accompanying the capture was nothing short of skin crawling and extraordinary.

All these years waiting.

No close calls.

No contact.

Then, there they were.

Those who took Mama. Mama and half of the world.

It was a mere myth.

Bedside stories.

Obscurity made real.

They were real.

I had always assumed they would come like hyenas. Cackling.

Or weird wildebeests grunting, snortling, salivating loudly. The drip, drip, drip of their saliva.

It was nothing of the sort. Deep clicks, clacks, deep vibrations that gave them away.

Their noises though ,their signals, their own weird form of communication wasn't bereft of voices.

The noises were part and parcel of the language they spoke, not the quintessence of their communication, but the noises were voices, all which were laced in their language.

THE LANGUAGE.

As soon as some of the words were heard, conveyed, offered, I was aware of the real-life danger; more so than working off of mere rumour and Papa's talk.

Working against and with a preprogrammed way to react to this type of situation, one that Papa had warned and trained me for.

The Language wasn't human.

It was not decipherable, but, communicated and felt; a language spoken by human mouths, but mouths from far beyond this pale.

  That was when I knew they had him.

They could have heard me, but I didn't listen. I

 was aware, but not to the degree my father listened.

If you listen, they come.

He listened, he must of... deliberately?

To determine where they were, to deter them from me and Greta? Was that why he dropped his tools?

Was it all an orchestration?

These kinds of thoughts plagued me.

I was only broken out of my first initial reveries because a little voice said,

"Doorwah...Doorwah...ungry...pwease...hun-hun-Greeeeeeeeeeeeee!" and that's when I had to listen.

Close off my mind.

Open my ears. To attune to the cellar. Our future home.

For what at that point was the foreseeable future.

Papa had taught me how to block out their noise whilst attenuating to our noise. Something that now I had to teach Greta.

I also had to be careful with Greta.

All these months of back chatting, arguing with Papa about how much we reveal to my simple-minded three-year-old sister.

Had I forced this? By wanting life's harshness and ruthlessness to strike out, to teach her some kind of lesson?

To force Papa's hand?

I was wracked with guilt. Trying to assign blame.

I breathed in. Deeply.

The cellar was musky but luckily with accompanying smell of tinctures, ointment, pickled jars, jams, fresh-ish blankets and clothes, it wasn't that bad.

It was breathable and not too bad.

I had smelt worse.

Far worse.

"There is no blame" Papa had told me, on the third year without Mama.

"It is their fault" I struck out, throwing wood into the firepit we were sat at, angrily.

Papa had come around to my side and hugged me.

I always felt safe in his bearlike embrace.

"There is no blame. If it happens it happens. Is it a life I want for you? No. Maybe the blame is mine? Don't forget it was my decision not to seek them out for forgiveness, Dor. But, in many ways, I don't blame them. I blame The Church. But never them. They are as they are.

As God or the Devil had them made.

That's the only way we are united in a sense.

The Lord willed this into happening.

We had no choice.

Neither did they.

We are all victims of The Church and their ways".

Down in the cellar, as much as I tried to believe this, I couldn't.

I grew angry at Father's admittance of being in the wrong. The Church wanted that. To admit fault means one is asking for forgiveness. No one should ask them for anything.

They worked for/or with the church.

They set out to trap people. Make them admit their supposed sins.

They had altered the world.

It was their way or no way.

These things saw The Church come into power.

Though the few we had passed or bumped into in our time in this current era of the world, there was always debates, opposing arguments, about admittance, acceptance, kowtowing, and maybe ultimately joining The Church.

Asking for forgiveness. Father knew the truth.

More than he had ever let on.

I learned far more without Papa, in these past few years myself, if and when we contacted the rest of the world not under the worldwide umbrella known only as The Church.

Papa only joined ranks and rendezvoused when previsions were low and he had to make trades of his tinctures and ointments for materials, tools, food, general supplies to maintain the hut.

But I loved being around these people, these people that were our people.

Though many arguments were made, debated, they still stuck to living off the land and not under The Church.

They were my new community, sometimes they felt like family.

But this bunch we usually met up in the Southern regions, were travelers, whereas Father never ventured further than he needed to.

Keeping to his forest and terrain.

Father never leaned towards joining, ever, much like he didn't ever consider joining The Church.

He was a nomad.

A nomad with priorities and those being his two children.

Many of the fellow travelers children had grown up to leave and make their own decisions, others had been lured and brainwashed to join the clergy, or whatever weird ranks they had at The Church.

Father had eluded them for far too long and spouted too much blasphemy to be saved.

Helped or hindered or guided them, whichever way people argued, or tried to excuse these other-worldly cretins and creeps and villains, I was not going to let them off that easy.

Nor let them in.

***

"That was..."

"Powerful?"

"Generic, and in its genericism it was totally new."

"Thank you."

"No, thank you."

"Where can we go from here?"

"Edit!"

"What?!"

"The work!"

"Doesn't it lose a certain vitality, then?"

"I do not think so."

"No, that completely contradicts the whole reason for this inclusion."

us

you + we = watered down prestige television shows.

you+ we = waterproof penis-extenders

you + we = entertaining Richard Ayoade with puppets

you + we = shady agents pushing their rock star ingenue onto wild auteur filmmakers, only to get complaints about the dick pics they had received.

you + we = means we.

you + we = means us.

You, the reader.

Us, the writer, director, producer, gallerist, programmer.

Us.
Us.
You.
You.
Us.
Us.
We.
We.

You.
Me.
No.
Limits.

To.

Our.

Bond.

Experiment.

Pretend.

Digital protrusions.

Lost causes.

101 box rooms filled with forgotten memories.

Loose limbs.

Jimmy open the baked bin tins.

The independent thinkers of our day and age died a horrible Netflix subscribed death.

                                             Us.
Us.
                                          You.
You.
                                             Us.

Us.

We.

We.

You.

Me.

No.

More.

Gods.

Death to the false salesmen dressed as a baseball
Daddio.

Collecting blood.

Extracting muse.

Poetry fucked.

Prose mangled.

Authorial voices lost to a variety of salty breeze-
screams.

No more.

No less.

We are you.

You are we.

we + you = us

The me/the you/the we.

Books unite us.

There is awkwardness in every gesture.

There is mania with every new neighbour you have to

suffer.

There is always shite between the tiles in the local

toilets.

There is always a lie on the tip of a junky's tongue.

There is always an always. There is never a forever.

No more blurbs.

No more reviews.

No more fandom.

No more.

No less.

Questioning and needling and un-liking posts

because

you're scared of the proverbial status quo.

No more.

You.

Me.

Us.

They.

Them.

Friends.

Lost.

Agonies written and encouraged onto canvas.

Pastels used as a rare exchange rate.

Big fonts.

Italic-licks.

Vehicle carnage salt licks.

Grain.

Lost novels.

Rare editions.

Approved elections made cancel culture a great
online

pastime.

The work is not important.

Everything is a major fail.

Only indie presses and authors.

No more.

Gatekeepers.

Support.

No.

One.

Trust.

Us.

Meaning, we.

Zak Ferguson

Author Bio:

Zak Ferguson is an Autistic experimental author/filmmaker/autistic noise-composer living in Brighton, UK. Zak is also the Co-Founder of the innovative, boundary-pushing Sweat Drenched Press.

Zak Ferguson

we + you = us